Roanoke County Public Library
Vinton Branch Library
800 East Washington Ave.
Vinton, VA 24179

NO LONGER
PROPERTY OF
ROANOKE COUNTY LIBRARY

ORSON SCOTT CARD

This special signed edition is limited to 1,000 numbered copies.

This is copy 463.

Hamlet's Father

Hamlet's Father

Orson Scott Card

Subterranean Press & Hatrack River 2011

Hamlet's Father
Copyright © 2009
by Orson Scott Card. All rights reserved.

Dust jacket and interior illustrations
Copyright © 2011 by Tom Kidd.
All rights reserved.

Interior design Copyright © 2011
by Desert Isle Design, LLC.
All rights reserved.

First Edition

ISBN
978-1-59606-269-6

Subterranean Press
PO Box 190106
Burton, MI 48519

www.subterraneanpress.com
www.hatrack.com

HAMLET'S FATHER SENT HIM TO the university at Heidelberg as soon as he turned fourteen. Even though he had to leave all his friends behind, Hamlet was glad to go.

It wasn't Denmark he wanted to leave. It was the castle at Elsinore; it was the throne that he would probably never occupy; it was Mother's endless sadness and infinite distance from him.

It was Father.

To be son of a king—it must sound so wonderful to boys with ordinary, nonregal fathers. The reality was far different.

Father was once as powerful as God, or so it seemed to Hamlet. Indeed, when the

Bishop discussed God, Hamlet couldn't see how there was any difference between God and Father. They were both all-knowing, all-powerful.

But gradually it became clear to Hamlet that Father, with his infinite knowledge and wisdom, had judged his only son and found him permanently wanting. It began when Hamlet was six, playing with his Companions—the sons of nobles or wealthy commoners, brought to the castle to study Latin with him and to learn the arts of war. Hamlet could hear Father preparing for the hunt with a visiting lord from Jutland and his retinue. How Hamlet begged to be taken along on such expeditions! The hounds were barking, the horses stamping and whinnying, and servants were shouting orders to each other. All the boys stopped in their game to listen, to yearn.

Then came Polonius, Father's lord chamberlain and the father of Laertes, one of Hamlet's favorites among the Companions. Hamlet felt a thrill of anticipation: Father had sent for his son to accompany him!

Hamlet's Father

Instead, Polonius called out to another of the Companions, Horatio, and beckoned to him.

There was no explanation. Horatio left. Soon after, the horses and hounds went away, and there was silence from the courtyard. In the garden where Hamlet played with his remaining friends, there was nothing but somberness, and games ended without ending, petering out for lack of interest.

Finally Hamlet ended up where he always went when he wanted to be alone—the graveyard behind the chapel. Hamlet had no fear of the dead—weren't they all his family and their faithful servants, or kings and queens from ancient lines that had withered away?—but the other boys were leery of the place, and Hamlet had long since reassured them that their duty to stay with him "at all times" did not include his graveyard visits. They were still officially "with him" if they remained in the garden. "All I do is rest and think," he said.

But that was not entirely true. Sometimes he dreamed. Sometimes he prayed. Sometimes he cried.

He was still in the graveyard when he heard the hunt return. He did not rush to join his Companions in greeting Father and the Earl of Jutland and his retinue. But he could not lie peacefully upon any of the graves now. He got up and began to pace. Then he climbed the apple tree nearest the ancient tomb of another family that once ruled in Elsinore but had been replaced by Grandfather, and tested himself to see if he was tall enough now to cling to a branch and swing himself onto the roof of the tomb. He quickly discovered that while he was definitely taller, he was also heavier, and bowed the branch lower, so he could only kick the wall of the tomb, not swing his legs up on top.

By the time he was big enough, he had become too big.

Angry, he let himself drop to the ground.

"The fruit has grown large and ugly this year," said a familiar voice—Yorick, the old jester.

"It's too early for apples."

"Then what kind of weather is it that drops ugly boys out of the sky?"

"I'm not ugly. Mother says I'm a very pretty little boy."

"Better to be ugly," said Yorick, and there was sadness in his voice.

"Why is that?" said Hamlet. "Pretty is always better."

"When you're older, if you're still pretty, then when you marry a woman you won't know whether she is marrying you for your pretty looks or because you're a prince."

"Why not both?"

"Why not neither?"

"I don't want to marry anybody," said Hamlet.

"But you will," said Yorick, "and you must be sure that she never knows you're pretty. Marry someone who lives far away. Let her think you're ugly as a toad. Then you'll be sure she's marrying you because of your royal blood."

"Why would I want that?"

"If she marries you because you're pretty, then when you get old like me she'll love some other young man. But if she marries you because you're a prince, then when you're old you'll still be prince—or king. So she'll keep on loving you."

"It's a good thing you're a fool," said Hamlet, "or I might believe you."

"It's always good not to believe me," said Yorick. "Ask your mother."

"Ask her what?"

"If she married your father because he's pretty." Then Yorick turned serious. "I'm sent to call you in. Your father doesn't know yet that you left your Companions, but he'd be angry if he knew. Don't get your friends in trouble."

Hamlet's Father

"I didn't tell them to leave the garden," said Hamlet. "They could have stayed."

"They all thought you would go to meet the hunt as well. And they can't go back and do what they should have done—they're in the castle now, and people are starting to ask where you are. Your mother sent me for you."

If he had said Polonius sent for him, Hamlet would not have gone—not till they sent soldiers for him, or Mother herself. But since it was Mother doing the sending, Hamlet went.

"And you're filthy," said Yorick. "Covered with the dust of the dead. Go wash your face or people will think you're a ghost."

"I will if there's warm water."

"If you need warm water to wash in, you'll never be man enough to be king."

"Cold water makes a king?" asked Hamlet scornfully.

"Cold water makes a king wise," said Yorick, "and in Denmark, only a wise man is clever enough to persuade the lords to make him king."

"Then why don't kings swim in the cold cold sea every day of the year?"

"Because," said Yorick, "only a fool would do that." Then he laughed and cackled and cavorted till Hamlet was laughing, too, and followed him toward the castle.

He stopped and washed at the same fountain that the soldiers used—it was an excuse to be near the foul-speaking men who smelled of horses and dogs and sweat and farts and ale; Hamlet adored them, and they liked him too. But there were none about right now, for Father had invited all the hunt to his supper, where they would share the hog that had been roasting all the long morning.

Yet Hamlet thought he heard someone speaking, and not inside the stables, where grooms would be caring for the horses, and not in the kennels, either, where the barksome dogs were being fed and petted. The voice came from around the corner of the great keep, and when Hamlet went toward the sound he realized it wasn't speech, it was someone crying.

It was Horatio. Hamlet knew his voice.

Hamlet made a noise, so Horatio would know someone was coming. Thus when Hamlet came around the corner, Horatio was not crying at all, though his eyes were red and his nose was red and a little snotty, as was his sleeve.

"How was the hunt?" asked Hamlet.

Horatio tried a little smile. "I'm sorry to go, when I know you wanted to."

"I don't mind," said Hamlet, though of course that was a complete lie.

"I asked your father why he didn't take you, but he only said, 'I take the one that's ready for the hunt.' I said, 'The Prince is ready,' but he had them hoist me up on his horse in front of him."

My place. He took my place.

"That's your place," said Horatio. "I'm sorry."

"How was the hunt?" asked Hamlet again. It wasn't Horatio's fault, he knew, so he didn't need apologies. But he still had to know what they actually *did* on this day's hunt. So he could think about it. Lying on a grave, he could remember a day that he didn't actually have, the day with Father on the hunt.

Horatio told about it, but he never got excited. And when it came to the kill, he couldn't say anything at all. "I saw a hart and two hinds astraddle the horses on the way home," he said. "And the Earl of Jutland had killed them all, so he was very proud and also grateful to your father for letting him take three from his deerpark."

"Father didn't kill any of them?" asked Hamlet.

"We got lost," said Horatio. "We didn't rejoin the hunt until on the way home. The Earl of Jutland wasn't going to take a deer without the King, but old Bearhand told him that the King wanted him to take three—one for himself, one for the King's house, and one to be cut up and shared with the poor."

"That was done like a Christian," said Hamlet.

"That's what they all said," said Horatio.

"You must have been sorry, though, to miss the kill."

Horatio almost sobbed again. "I was very sorry to miss it," he said, as soon as he had control of his emotions again.

"I hope next time I can go," said Hamlet.

But Horatio said nothing at all. Hamlet took him by the shoulder and got him to wash his face, and by the time they got into the castle no one could tell that Horatio had been crying.

If it had been only the once, Hamlet might have forgiven his father the shame of taking someone else before him. But as the months and years went by, and all the other boys were taken on hunts and other expeditions, and Hamlet never, it became more than a mere disappointment, more than a shame. It was Father's way of repudiating him, Hamlet could see that. Whatever it is that Father valued in a boy, Hamlet did not have it.

Not that Hamlet thought for a moment that the other boys were actually better. Hamlet always took pride in never allowing them to allow him to win at any of their contests. When he lost, he took it without shame or anger, and no one reported on the outcome to Father or Polonius, lest they interfere and punish someone for outdoing the Prince. Thus, whenever Hamlet won, he knew that his victory was real. He was the fastest runner, save Laertes; he was the best at Latin, save Rosencrantz; he was the strongest at wrestling, save Guildenstern, and then only on some days could the older boy throw him down.

At one thing, though, Hamlet was the best save *nobody,* and that was the sword. It was a natural gift—the armsmaster said so. Right from the start, Hamlet had a way of sensing just where his opponent's sword was going to be. With training, he began to understand this gift and refine it; by the time he was twelve he could watch a match with the swordmaster of Elsinore and name for him all the moves and tell what the losing swordsman should have done. It was all clear to him, all parts of swordsmanship—the stance, the flow, the point, the shaft, the heft, the guards, the parries, the slashes, the lunges. Left hand or right, taller opponent or heavier or shorter or lither, it didn't matter, Hamlet could see what they were doing just a split second before they did it, and even if he spent half a match dancing away from a longer-armed opponent, no one ever laid point or blade on Hamlet's body.

Whether he had a gift for it or not, however, Hamlet took every activity seriously. Even when Mother brought the boys in and began their training as pages, teaching them orders of precedence and heraldry, and the meaning of various dishes and how each day's dinner was the product of months of planning in garden, field, orchard, sty, pen, coop, and, above all, larder. How do you know when you need to hunt? How long must meat age? What spices preserve a sausage, and which merely make it palatable? What should be smoked and what should be salted down for winter? How many calves, lambs, and goslings should be allowed to live, and how long?

Why should I know this, Mother?

"Because you are Prince, my darling boy, and you have to know at a glance if your people are rich or poor, if they need relief or help from you, or if they are prosperous enough to be well and deeply taxed. You need to know if you have food enough for the men you keep around you, and you need to know how to order them—and the lords as well—so that quarreling is kept down and merit is always named and known."

So Hamlet set out to become the best at this as well, so that by the age of thirteen he was able to greet every visitor graciously by name and inquire after his family, and address all men by their right titles and afford them their right recognition.

Hamlet's Father

The more he learned, though, the more Hamlet realized that his father was not, in fact, very good at any of it. He treated powerful men of ancient family as if they mattered little, and then inadvertently showed too much favor to one who had not earned it and had no right to it.

Like the way Father treated his brother, Uncle Claudius, as if he were the royal fool instead of old Yorick. Holding him up to ridicule in front of visitors. Yet Claudius bore it with dignity, showing neither rancor nor eagerness to please. He bore it as if he had been afforded great honor, as he deserved, being also a prince and son of one king and brother of another.

It had seemed natural and funny, back when Hamlet was little and Prince Claudius was still not yet fully a man. Beardless, too thin, gawky—of course Father teased him.

But by the time Hamlet began to get his growth at age thirteen, Claudius was as strong and sturdy a man, as fine-looking, as sharp-minded as any lord. As the King himself. Or perhaps stronger, sturdier, finer-looking, and sharper-minded than the King. To Hamlet, long used to his father's public disdain of him, Uncle Claudius seemed more kingly than the king. And yet still Father publicly shamed him.

Didn't Father see that it made himself, not Claudius, look ridiculous? Oh, people laughed, because it was plain the King wanted them to. But Hamlet saw that when the japery was over, people cast looks of pity at Uncle Claudius. And more than that—more than once Hamlet saw lords and great men of the realm conferring quietly with Uncle Claudius, and with great solemnity, as if they discussed matters grave and stately. This they would not do if they thought Uncle Claudius a fool.

Hamlet even said so once, when he and Laertes were alone on the riverbank after a long swim. The other Companions were still in the water, and could not hear them.

"I wish Uncle Claudius were my father," said Hamlet.

Laertes turned on him savagely—angrily, even. "Do you wish your mother were an adulteress then? Or do you wish *her* not to be your mother, either?"

"I was just...wishing," said Hamlet. "Father hates me, so I might as well not be his son."

Laertes looked out across the water, his face dark with—what, anger? "There is no boy happier than the King's own son," he said.

"Then all the boys in the world must be sad all the time," said Hamlet, "because I am. No matter how hard I work to become the Prince he wants me to be—"

"And Prince Claudius admires you? Is that it? Instead of becoming what your father wants you to be, you'd rather have a father who is satisfied with what you already are? What kind of king will you be, then? The kind who surrounds himself with toadies who always tell him that he's wonderful and brilliant? Or the kind of king who surrounds himself with men who are wiser and stronger than he is, so he can use their wisdom and strength for the good of the kingdom?"

Hamlet always hated it when Laertes got into a mood to preach sermons. It was a trait he shared with his father; Polonius was so full of platitudes they slopped out of him like milk from a swinging bucket.

"If the king surrounds himself with men who are wiser and stronger," said Hamlet, "then why is he king, and not those men?"

"Be careful," said Laertes. "There's only so much treason I can listen to without having to behead myself."

"I'm not talking about my lord Father anymore," said Hamlet. "I'm speaking of myself. I know our history. Many a son has been passed over when he wasn't worthy to be king. If my Father shows such disrespect for me, then why would the earls look for virtues that my father didn't find in me?"

Hamlet's Father

"And if he kept you with him as his constant companion," said Laertes, "then you'd learn only the way to be a king like him, instead of a better one."

"Do you really think he shuns me so I'll be a better king?"

In answer, Laertes got up and plashed out into the water.

Hamlet watched him, thinking two things:

Why is there no one I can talk to about the things that matter most to me?

How beautiful he is.

They are all beautiful, Hamlet thought, looking at his Companions as they swam and splashed and dived. Strong and vigorous, lovely of face. As if my father chose them for me to make sure I never thought of myself as strongest, most vigorous, or handsomest. As if he wanted to make sure my opinion of myself stayed forever as low as his opinion of me.

What kind of scrawny, weepy, screaming, drooling, pissing, puking, shitting, flatulent wretch was I as a baby, that he hated me from the moment I was born?

"No more or less of those things than any other baby," Yorick told him, on the day Hamlet dared to ask him the question. "And you still do all those things, just like everybody else. All that's changed is that you now know when and where to do them."

"All I have of my father is his name," said Hamlet.

"What if his greatest gift," said Yorick, "is to give you no gift?"

"Which is the greater fool," answer Hamlet, "the fool who thinks he's wise, or the fool who knows he's a fool and plays the part?"

"The fool who knows he's a fool is wise, and therefore no fool," said Yorick. "But the greater fool is the wise man who does not know he is wise, for then he follows not his own counsel."

"Where did you learn *that* bit of wisdom?"

"From Polonius."

"I thought so."

"It's one of my duties in the castle of Elsinore," said Yorick. "To clean up after my betters. I mop up the excess wisdom that drops upon the floor, stew it into a soup, soup it into a stew, and then serve it back to my betters as a fine feast of foolery."

"Better to steep it into soap," said Hamlet, "so we could wash with it."

"How can wisdom go into soap, since soap is full of lyes?"

"Sometimes to lie is wise."

"And sometimes to ask why is a lie," said Yorick. "So lies are wise and whys are lies."

"You pile so many meanings together that none of it means anything," said Hamlet.

"Which is why I'm still employed here at Elsinore. If anyone ever found a meaning in what I said, I'd soon be dead."

An observation that pretended to be mere jest, but which Hamlet knew to be true. Yorick might be a fool by trade, but even he could see that Father was not much of a king.

HAMLET WAS AT sword practice, the last time he saw his father alive. He no longer practiced with his Companions, for he had long since proven himself their master and had nothing to learn from them, even with old Bernardo, the Italian swordmaster, watching to criticize. These days his arms were long enough to practice with men—with strong soldiers who had wielded sabers, cutlasses, and great two-handed swords in battle, and with lordlings who had dueled with rapiers and remained alive to tell of it.

They practiced with nocked and dull-edged blades, their bodies covered with heavy padding—except that Hamlet wore almost none, because it hindered him. So when Father came out to watch, Hamlet was afraid he'd rail at Bernardo for risking royal blood by letting him duel without enough protection.

But that was Mother who worried about him; Father gave no sign that he cared one way or another.

When the practice was done, and Bernardo had his man gather the practice swords into the wheelbarrow, Father did the thing he never did. He called his son by name.

"Hamlet!"

It made him tremble inwardly, to hear his name in that voice. At once he turned and trotted to his father; he would have run full out, except the distance was so short.

"My lord Father," said Hamlet, falling to one knee.

"Oh get up," said Father. "Why should a servant waste time washing those leggings because you had to kneel in the mud?"

So there was no honor intended when Father called him.

"Your mother's been pestering me for months that we've run out of useful teachers for you. So we're sending you to the university in Heidelberg. Try not to turn yourself into something useless—clerks make poor kings."

As if Father knew what a good king was. "Which of my Companions may I take with me?"

"I'm dissolving your Companions and bringing them all directly into my service," said Father. "You'll take none of them—only enough servants and men-at-arms that you don't embarrass Denmark by appearing paltry compared to the German princes who attend there."

"As my lord father wishes," said Hamlet. "When is my journey to begin?"

"Tomorrow," said Father. "As I told your mother, once I agree to let you go, what's the point of keeping you here?"

Hamlet bowed. It was bitter, to hear how Father still despised him; but he couldn't help but be glad that there would be no waiting. It would be hard to leave home—to leave his Companions, especially Laertes and Horatio, and he would miss Mother. And Yorick. But it would be good to go somewhere else, to see something of the world. To be away from the darkness of Father's disregard for him.

None of the Companions were with him at supper, and Hamlet realized that Father was punishing him. Even though Hamlet hadn't asked to go anywhere, Father had apparently disapproved of his going, and so he would be barred from saying good-bye to his friends.

Then, after supper, he walked on the battlements of the castle to take his last look at the lingering sunset of early summer. The sun spread its pink light along a row of clouds on the western horizon, over the low hills of Zealand. On the eastern side, darkness gathered on the Swedish side of the Oresund, as if night had to work up a great deal more strength before it could leap the straits and land in Denmark.

Someone was walking on the battlements. But staying in the shadows.

For one moment Hamlet felt a thrill of fear as he thought: This is how an assassin might come.

But in a moment his stealthy visitor came out into the open, and it was Laertes, not a murderer. Hamlet had to laugh at his own fear. "I thought for a moment you were someone who had come to kill me," he said. "The way you stayed in the shadows." As if anyone would find Hamlet worth killing.

"I hid because your father forbade any of the Companions to speak with you."

"Of course he did," said Hamlet. "For fear you'd make me feel as though I might be missed."

"You will be," said Laertes. "More than you know."

"Father's taking you into his own service. Men now, not Companions to a boy prince."

"It's an honor I did not want."

"Nor did I want to be a prince and get sent off to Heidelberg," said Hamlet. "Sometimes we just have to be patient with inconvenient honors."

Hamlet's tone had been jesting, but the darkness that came upon Laertes' face was almost painful. "What is it?"

"Hamlet, I beg you, before you go, ask your father to send me away. To France. My mother's brother is there, lord of a small holding on the border between Normandy and the Ile-de-France. Father will never ask—he's too much the courtier. But if you ask—"

"Laertes, when did you ever see my father listen to me and do something that I asked him?"

Laertes turned away, his face a mask of despair. "I know," he said.

"Besides," said Hamlet, "how can you go, when your sister Ophelia is beginning to need the protection of a good sword?"

"Ophelia's in no danger from any man in Elsinore," said Laertes.

"If you want a favor from my father, perhaps you ought to enlist the help of the person who was able to persuade him to send me away."

"And who was that?"

"The queen my mother," said Hamlet.

"Queen Gertrude doesn't even know my name," said Laertes.

"Then let's go to her, and I'll introduce you."

It took some persuasion, but Laertes was so desperate to leave Elsinore that at last he trailed along behind Hamlet through the halls of the castle. Finally they came to the Queen's chambers, which were on the south side of the castle, overlooking the practice grounds. How often, wondered Hamlet, has she watched from here as I bested every opponent with my sword? If she ever did, he had not heard of it.

But Mother, at least, knew he was alive. She had taught him much, and thought enough of him to think he might benefit from more education. She cared enough to persuade Father of it. That was more than the nothing he got from Father.

Hamlet knelt before her and she took his hands in hers, then glanced up at Laertes, who waited just inside the door of her rooms.

"Father isn't coming here, is he?" asked Hamlet.

"Small chance of that," said Mother cheerfully. "Why have you brought me Polonius's boy?"

"To ask your help for him," said Hamlet. "He wants to go live with a cousin in France, but his father won't plead for him to be released from the King's service in order to do it."

"The King's service?" asked Mother.

So she hadn't known that his Companions were being taken directly into the King's own Guard. And when he explained it, she frowned and reached out a hand to Laertes. "One would have thought," she said to the boy, "that you served him well enough already."

She stood, and saw that Laertes was already as tall as she was, and laughed. "Well, it seems you're determined to be taller than your father."

"I should be," said Laertes. "My mother was."

"I think that if you bide only a little while, my dear husband will have no further use of you."

Laertes looked away. "If I live so long."

"Live," said Mother. "I command it."

"Then I'll obey," said Laertes, but it didn't sound like playful banter; he sounded sad.

"I'll speak to the King about releasing all the Companions. I think that all your fathers would be glad to have you back, since you are no longer with the Prince. You are all the sons of barons, and can't be commanded like the sons of commoners."

Laertes gave one short bark of a laugh.

Hamlet's Father

"Your service," said Mother, "is not the King's to take, but rather your fathers' to offer."

"Do you doubt that my father would offer me?" said Laertes.

"I doubt he would offer you willingly," said Mother. "But no, I do not doubt that he'd give you over to the King's service. So I will frame it to my dear husband in such a way as to keep him from holding on to you just because your father dares not stand up to him. But when it happens, then get yourself to France as quickly as you can, and stay out of sight, because my dear husband will be in a snappish mood for some months to come, if I know him at all."

"I thank you with all my heart, my lady queen," said Laertes. "Know that I am forever in *your* service, if you ever have need of me."

"I take that pledge of honor most seriously, Laertes," said the Queen. "Now leave me with my son. I *will* say good-bye to him, as my dear husband knew perfectly well I would do, even though he commanded me not to and I promised faithfully to obey him."

Hamlet had no idea what it meant, for her to claim on the one hand that Laertes' word of honor was worthy of respect, and on the other hand that she had given her own oath to Father with the full intent of breaking it. Women were not to be understood, it was as simple as that.

As soon as Laertes had slipped out and closed the door, Mother rose to her feet and embraced him. "You're a better son than your father and I had any right to hope for," she said.

"It's a well-kept secret from my father."

"You do not know what you do not know," said Mother. "Your father has loved you better than you think."

Then she turned away and said, "Come out and bid your nephew Godspeed."

To Hamlet's surprise, Uncle Claudius emerged from behind a tapestry. "Your uncle and I were conferring about a matter

23

of some estates in Holstein," Mother explained. "But since my dear husband has forbidden him to take an interest in the royal lands, I can only get his advice by stealth. When you knocked on the door, I commanded him to hide."

Claudius stepped forward and held out his hand. "I'm sorry you'll be leaving us," he said. "I've taken much pleasure in watching you play with your opponents on the practice field."

So *someone*, at least, had been watching. "Thank you, my lord," said Hamlet.

"He called me 'my lord,'" said Claudius to Mother with a smile. "Even though he's one of the three in this land who don't owe me any honorifics. You've raised him to be gracious."

"No one raised him," said Mother. "He is what he is because of the nature God gave him, and nothing he got from parents or teachers."

"I learned everything from you, Mother," said Hamlet, "except war."

"Ah," she said. "But war is the all in all, isn't it? That's what separates princes from other folks—the power to lead great numbers of men out to kill people, without fear of reprisals from God."

"No man is above the judgment of God," said Hamlet. "Not even kings—you taught me so yourself."

"You have me confused with the archbishop," said Mother. "I don't teach anybody about God. He and I are little acquainted of late, and I wouldn't presume to speak for him."

"Whom are you little acquainted with?" asked Claudius. "You are unclear. The archbishop or his master?"

"I referred to neither," said Mother, smiling. "I spoke of God."

Claudius laughed lightly and moved away toward the window.

So Mother thought the archbishop's "master" was not God. Then who did she think owned the man? Father? Or the devil?

"There's so much you never taught me," said Hamlet.

Hamlet's Father

"Or me, for that matter," said Claudius confidingly, as if he and Hamlet were brothers in an old conspiracy. "Ever since your father became king, the only teacher I've had is your mother. But she holds back the juiciest bits of information for herself. She's afraid we'll become too powerful, if we know what she knows."

"*I* don't even know what I know," said Mother. "I don't dare ask myself a single question for fear I'll tell me an answer that I can't afford to hear."

Claudius laughed again, but Hamlet didn't understand the jest, if it *was* a jest.

"God be with you, Mother," said Hamlet. "I'll try to make you proud of me by all I do in Heidelberg."

"I'm glad of that," said Mother. "I'll be waiting for you when you come back. I'm proud of you. I'm proud of the man I see you ready to become."

"And the king," said Claudius.

"What about him?" asked Mother.

"The king that your son is nearly ready to become," said Claudius. "I spoke of that."

"My father your brother is still a young man," said Hamlet. "It will be a long while before Denmark needs another king."

Claudius seemed about to say something else, a bitter remark that twisted his mouth a little; but Mother held up her hand and he did not say it. But Hamlet knew what would have been said—that Denmark *needs* another king right now, but isn't likely to get one. It bothered him that Claudius and Mother seemed to speak freely between themselves about Father's shortcomings as king. There was much to be said on that score, of course, but it was unseemly for the King's wife and brother to scorn him, even privately.

Hamlet put it out of his mind. Claudius and Mother had both praised him, and Hamlet held his uncle in such high esteem that he knew that *his* respect should be enough.

But it wasn't.

He bade them good-bye and returned to his chamber, where his clothing for the next day's journey was already laid out, and all his other clothing packed away in trunks and bags that littered the floor of the room. He expected to lie awake, dreaming or fretting about Heidelberg, or mourning for the childhood that had just ended so abruptly. But he fell asleep instead, and if he dreamed, he remembered nothing of it in the morning. By noon he was aboard a ship, with the oarsmen pulling strongly into the currents of the strait, heading northward to round the coasts of Jutland and bring him, eventually, up the Rhine to the Neckar, where Heidelberg awaited him.

WHAT IS THERE to say of Heidelberg? It was the happiest time of Hamlet's life. Though at first he was homesick—how could he help but be, so far from the sea, so far from the friends he had known from childhood on, so far from his mother? But he soon found new friends, and of a different sort than he had ever known before.

There were few lordlings in Heidelberg, save of course the local dignitaries. He paid his visits and gave them their due, but made it clear he was at Heidelberg to be an honest student, and would have little time for hunting or dancing or the other pastimes of the nobility.

And he made good on his word. He found himself far behind many others in Latin and Greek, for his fellow students were no hand-picked firstborn sons of nobles, they were the second, third, and later sons of barons and knights, who had no prospects of inheriting their family lands and therefore had nowhere to turn but to the church, as well as the promising children of tradesmen looking to raise their families' stations through a lofty church appointment.

Hamlet's Father

There were few who had any interest in swordplay or other games of war; they pounded their heads against their books and conversed continually in Latin, arguing theology from Augustine and Aquinas, as well as philosophy from the Greeks, while reciting poetry from Homer to Virgil, with many a stop at Ovid and other racier poets along the way.

At first, feeling uncomfortably ill-prepared, Hamlet made a show of carrying his sword with him wherever he went, and he managed to take offense in several of the pubs frequented by students. But he so quickly disarmed his few opponents that there was no sport in it; nor was anyone impressed, at least not among the students of the sort he wanted to befriend. Within a few months, he hung the sword on a peg on the wall of his rooms and carried books like everyone else.

He soon found that the road to acquaintanceship was to spend his money, not on fine foods, but on precious books. He found out from the best professors what books they most coveted, and then endowed the appropriate monasteries with funds enough to procure copies at the earliest date. It took a few months for the first of these books to arrive, but when they did, he made a point of forbidding the professors to tell how they had obtained them. As he well knew, this absolutely guaranteed that his generosity would be celebrated throughout the university, along with a reputation for modesty.

Meanwhile, he paid poorer students to tutor him and practiced his Latin as once he had practiced with the sword. Soon enough, though he never lost his Danish accent, he was fluent enough not only to be understood when he spoke and to make sense of most of what he read, but also to be able to overhear others' conversations, without knowing the topic, and understand them. He was, in a word, fluent, and it felt to him as if the whole world had opened its gates to him. He made friends, not only with young men of the armiger class, but also with the sons of tradespeople, a sort of person he would never have known in Denmark, except to order their obedience. And by the second year he found that some of his best friends were men long dead, whose books spoke to his heart with such brilliance and power that he revered them more than any living men he had ever known.

For four years he studied, and if he had not been the heir to the throne of Denmark, so that he could not take holy orders, he would have been offered many a prestigious post; even with his high birth, he was invited to come to Rome to study there, and gave it serious consideration for a while, though eventually he decided it would not be wise to be seen in Denmark as a tool of the Pope, which would imply too close a connection to the Holy Roman Empire, which always loomed on the southern borders of Denmark, despite its ups and downs. The Danish earls would need to be assured of his loyalty to Denmark and his fealty to no one but God and the Danish people.

Out of his father's shadow, he was happy. There were people who loved and admired him, not for his birth or his beauty (though neither was ignored), but for his mind and his wit and his loyalty and his kindness. He liked being loved, and he looked forward to the day when he would govern Denmark with generosity and rectitude. "Even as ye have done it unto the least of these, ye have done it unto me": He intended this to be the guiding principle of his reign, and aspired that someday he might be remembered, not as King Hamlet the Great, but rather as Hamlet the Good or Hamlet the Just. He would not go a-conquering; he would labor to keep the peace and help his kingdom prosper, unburdened by a luxurious court or excessive military adventures.

Then came the messenger with a letter from Elsinore that could not await the normal post. He had hastened from Denmark on horseback, with a military escort as befitted the message.

Hamlet's Father

"Hamlet, my son, your father has died, and you are needed at home. I send with this letter money enough for you to settle your debts if they are not unreasonable. Please come home at once." It was from his mother, who continued to style herself Queen Gertrude, though of course she would only bear that title until Hamlet married.

"Does this mean you're king now?" asked one of his professors, when he stopped to tell the news before he left.

"Not in Denmark," said Hamlet. "Though I'm the likeliest heir, the earls can choose from any of the lords. I must win their hearts to be considered. They hardly know me now. The last they saw of me I was a boy."

"So your kings are elected, like the Holy Roman Emperor?"

"Yes—but then we have more power, once we're chosen."

"More power than the Emperor?"

"Our country is smaller, of course, but our freedom to choose is greater, so that we can make decisions with less need to look over our shoulders."

"I know of no man readier to be a king," said the professor. "Plato once longed for a king like you, who was philosopher first. We are Christians; we want our kings to be philosophers *and* saints."

"I'm no saint," said Hamlet. "But I hope I will disappoint my people in neither wisdom nor virtue—nor strength and courage in battle."

"I know nothing of you as a soldier," said the professor. "But I know you to be fierce in argument."

"Here I've been gentle with my hands and fierce with my speech," said Hamlet. "At home I'll need to reverse that, for we Danes are still a violent people, when the need arises. And it arises too often for our own good."

"Then take that sword of yours off the peg on your wall. I hope you haven't lost any of your ability."

Hamlet laughed. "Who remembers now that I ever thought myself a swordsman?"

"We all remember, Prince Hamlet, though we don't speak of it. You bested the finest swordsmen in Heidelberg, who made a point of provoking you in the public houses."

Hamlet was surprised. "I thought it was I who was too quick to take offense, and that my opponents were all unskilled, so that it did me no honor to fight them."

The professor only laughed again. "There was even talk of the wealthier students paying for a mercenary to come and teach you manners. But then you put your sword away, and they ceased to fear for their lives. It was widely rumored that you had killed half of Denmark, and that's why you were sent here."

"I've never killed a man, sir," said Hamlet.

"And never will, God willing," said the professor.

Hamlet gave the messenger and his men a day to rest, while he settled all of his accounts; there were few debts to pay, since he had lived simply, having sent home all but one of his servants after the first year. His amusements had not been of the expensive kind, and the books he bought and gave away were paid for in advance.

It was an uneventful journey, and more than once he wished he could have gone by sea, which could scarcely have been slower, since it would have been a voyage down, not up, the Rhine, and then over sea. But the ship that came for him would not have made such good time with the news of his father's death; haste in the sending had been chosen over haste in the return. And so he rode, using the evenings and mornings to exercise and bring himself back into fighting trim. By the time they neared the borders of Denmark, he felt like he was nearly back to being himself with the sword, and he had made friends of all the soldiers in his guard. He even wondered, though he said nothing of it, whether some of these men might not be worthy of elevation to the King's Guard, should he be chosen king.

Hamlet's Father

Then came word from another messenger, sent to intercept him on the way, that even though Hamlet's father had not yet been buried—they awaited Hamlet's arrival to seal the body in its tomb—the earls had met and, without awaiting Hamlet's return, had chosen the new king.

Claudius. Uncle Claudius was king now.

It was the worst possible news. Hamlet had assumed that if the earls chose someone else, it would be an old man, who would function more as regent until Hamlet came fully of age, ready in the eyes of all to assume the throne. But Claudius was not that much older than Hamlet himself, and if he lived his three score and ten, Hamlet would be sixty years old before the throne would be available, and by then Claudius would surely have children of his own.

The blow was devastating, but not for the reason that others might have supposed. Indeed, it surprised Hamlet himself how very little he cared about the fact that he would not be king. Though he had spent his life preparing for the crown, he realized that in Heidelberg he had gained something that he loved more than the honor or power of rule. If Claudius wore the crown, then perhaps he would allow Hamlet to remain at court to advise him; or perhaps he would send Hamlet abroad as ambassador; or perhaps he would gift him with lands of his own. With any of these Hamlet would be content. But another possibility entered his mind: If he were neither king nor heir, perhaps he *could* take holy orders and live his life among books and professors. So even though it was wrenching to turn his mind to many possible futures once unthought-of, it did not bring him any unhappiness, not really.

No, what devastated him was the other news: That even as the funeral preparations were under way, Claudius had asked his brother's widow, Hamlet's mother, to marry him.

It had not crossed his mind that his mother would wish to remarry. But now he had to think of who she really was: a young woman, not yet thirty-five years of age, young enough to bear children. Claudius was younger than she was by eight years at least, but what of that? He was King. What woman wouldn't want to be married to the King?

But *Mother*? Hamlet had never thought of her as ambitious. She had endured Father's slighting treatment of her for all of Hamlet's life. He always thought that it was for his sake that she lived; it had never occurred to him that she might have loved being Queen so much that she cared little who sat the throne, as long as she sat beside him.

Unworthy thoughts—he tried to drive them from his mind. And to the men who were with him, he betrayed no doubt or disappointment. Indeed, he knew they would remark upon it to all, that when he heard of Uncle Claudius's elevation to the throne, Prince Hamlet's response was immediately to smile and say, "He's the best man in Denmark; the earls have chosen well." None would hear him utter a word of complaint. And if some thought that his cheerfulness was hiding the bitterness of broken hopes, let them.

There was another part of him, though, something deep inside that had a different reason for concealing his thoughts from all men. It was a recognition that he did not know Claudius all that well—hadn't he learned from his studies that only God could truly know the hearts of men? What if Claudius thought that Hamlet was, not his beloved nephew, but a bitter rival? Wouldn't Hamlet then have reason to fear his uncle? And wouldn't a pretense of loyalty and happiness be his best protection? For if he showed even the slightest trace of sullenness, if he even allowed himself to seem ill...

In the few days of riding after they crossed the borders into Denmark, though, Hamlet learned that feigning cheerfulness was a hard duty to perform. It wore him down. It wore him out. And besides, the men knew him too well: They had seen him quiet, thoughtful, even stern of face as he thought his thoughts.

Now to have him full of nothing but smiles would look so false and unconvincing that King Claudius, hearing report of it, would quickly decide that it was insincere, meant to conceal something dark and bitter.

No, the protective mask Hamlet wore would need to be something closer to his natural disposition: solitary, thoughtful, even brooding. He had been sharp of wit at school, a good comrade, but he had also been earnest and serious, and often quiet, seeking the company of books or his own thoughts. Like when he was a child and lingered in the graveyard, seeking to be alone for hours at a time. His own natural temper would be his best disguise.

"I can't pretend," he said to the men around him. "I've tried this whole journey to show my faith in God, not to grieve for my father's passing. A good Christian must be cheerful in the face of death, having a certainty of a glorious resurrection for himself and all those he loves best. But I can't lie to God, so why should I lie to you? My faith is too weak. I grieve for my father's death, and I won't pretend otherwise."

The men listened, nodding, sympathetic. The messenger even dared to commiserate. "May not a good Christian mourn for the loss of company, even if the dead have gone to heaven?"

"He may," Hamlet answered solemnly, and took the conversation no farther. For he had no wish to lie to these men any more than he had to. He did not love his father. Hamlet's only grief was that now he would never have a chance to earn his father's love and respect. And since it was unlikely he would ever have achieved such an apotheosis, it wasn't cause for that much grieving. Denmark was better off without Father as King. And better off, no doubt, without his brooding, scholarly son as King after him. God had ordained that Claudius be King; Mother that Claudius be her new husband; Hamlet would be content with all, so long as he could be allowed to return to his books and his philosophy as soon as possible after the funeral and the wedding.

He would not even begrudge Mother and Uncle Claudius their happiness. There was no blood relation between Claudius and Mother, after all. And didn't the Bible command that a man take his brother's widow to wife, to raise up progeny to his brother? Of course, that was only if the dead brother had no sons.

It was not a matter of legalisms. God had taken Father away from Denmark, away from Mother, away from them all. Whatever dark and brooding spirit had kept Father from showing genuine love to him or Mother, he was gone now, and with him the shadows he had cast in their lives. They were all free, and Hamlet most of all, for instead of having to bear the royal burden Father had borne so badly for all these years, he could live his life as he saw fit.

OF ALL HAMLET'S companions, only Horatio sought him out when he returned. This was hardly surprising—while Hamlet was in Heidelberg, Guildenstern had inherited his father's estates, and Rosencrantz had gone to live with him and help spend his money while waiting for his own father to die. Laertes was in France; he had been sent for, but not with the same urgency as Hamlet, since the dead King had not been his father. The others were sons of lesser barons, whose fathers could not afford to keep them at court once the king stopped paying for their upkeep as Companions.

But if Horatio was his only friend left in Elsinore, he was enough, at least for now. In some ways Horatio was still a boy, for to Hamlet all the practicing for war and death was a child's game, now that he had become a man of thoughts and words. In other ways, though, Hamlet was in awe of him, for Horatio had grown to be a strong man, looking older than his nineteen years, with an easy manner and a confidence born of strength—Horatio had nothing to fear.

It was Horatio who told him that the kingdom was secretly arming for war. In Norway, Fortinbras had recently succeeded to his father's throne, and anyone who was not a fool knew that he would, at the first opportunity, attempt to avenge his father's defeat at Denmark's hands fifteen years ago. There were lost lands that Fortinbras would want to reclaim, and the death of his old enemy, Hamlet's father, would be taken as an opportunity.

"So that's why the barons gave the throne to my uncle so quickly," said Hamlet.

"We're bound to have war this summer," said Horatio, "though no one speaks of it openly. In case Fortinbras wavers, there's no reason to provoke him by making known our own preparations for war. Better to keep the peace for another season."

"But we *do* prepare."

"Well, we do *now*. Your late father, God rest his soul, insisted that he had nothing to fear from Norway. 'I beat the father; the son won't dare attack while I'm alive.'" His imitation of Hamlet's father was nearly perfect—Horatio had the deep voice to bring it off.

"And now he's not alive," said Hamlet.

"He may have thought that he could easily defeat an untried boy who studied with the clerics in Heidelberg," said Horatio, winking. "You and I know that you're as skilled at the arts of war as any man, but Fortinbras had no idea."

"A war is not a duel," said Hamlet. "The barons were right to give the throne to my uncle, at a time like this."

"I'll not quarrel with their choice of a king," said Horatio. "Nor even with their haste in choosing. But you would have been a fine king, up to the challenge, and you may be yet."

"No talk of that," said Hamlet. "Even between the two of us, my friend. I have no ambition that should make my uncle mistrust me, but any speculation about my future will make him find disloyalty where there is none."

"You don't fear good Uncle Claudius, do you?" asked Horatio.

"The throne changes a man. I haven't seen him privately since I came back, and only twice at public ceremonies. He's busy—I attribute his ignoring me to that. But it might as easily be a dread of what he'll find in me. I'm the son of his new wife—that makes me the most dangerous man in the kingdom, if I choose to be, because it would be all the harder to strike me down if I undertook some sort of treason. No, Horatio, the best place for me is far from Denmark, and in circumstances where I'm not seen as a threat. I think there's a monastery in my future." And then he added, for no particular reason, "Perhaps in Rome."

"I don't see you becoming a priest," said Horatio.

"Not a *good* one," said Hamlet. "Taking orders and being a good father confessor are two different matters. A son of a king can hardly be a parish priest. But there might be a bishopric for me somewhere."

"And some day a red cap," said Horatio. "And someday Pope!"

"There's no place for ambition in the Church," said Hamlet.

"Oh ho," said Horatio, "so you *are* still a child."

"*I* have no ambition, anyway," said Hamlet. "I love my books as I once loved the sword."

"Have you slain any opponents in bookish duels?"

"I've slain no one with the sword, either, so both scores are even, at zero."

"When scholars duel, do they pitch the books like stones? Or bring them down on their opponent's head like a battleaxe?"

"Neither," said Hamlet, laughing. "We drive them into the other man's ear like a dagger, piercing his brain, which must find an argument to thrust it out again, before he bleeds to death."

"So books draw blood?"

"Scholars don't have blood flowing in their veins," said Hamlet. "When they're wounded, they bleed logic, and when all of it is gone, their brains die, and they become…soldiers."

Horatio pantomimed being pierced by an arrow through the heart. "Look! I'm pierced through, but I have no logic to bleed with!"

The joke had gone far enough, though, and Hamlet spoke earnestly: "You've always been my wisest friend."

"A deadly insult to Laertes, then. He was always proud of being the smartest one."

"No one is prouder of his wisdom than a fool," said Hamlet, holding up one finger in a parody of Polonius reciting a maxim.

"Are you quoting someone? Is that a translation from Latin?"

"I was imitating Laertes' father," said Hamlet.

"I'm glad you told me," said Horatio. "Because otherwise I wouldn't have known it."

"Speaking of Laertes…"

"Ophelia is still unmarried. Waiting for you, they say."

"Waiting for me to what?"

"To pay attention to her. To court her. Hamlet, don't tell me you didn't know how Polonius always hoped she'd marry you when you came of age."

"That was back when I had a crown in my future," said Hamlet.

"That might change the father's mind, but the daughter looks with different eyes."

Hamlet shook his head. "Having a wife is often taken by the Church as a discouragement to ordination."

"Do you really mean to live a life of celibacy?"

"I have all the ordinary lusts of the flesh," said Hamlet. "But to me, a woman is much like a pudding: when you're hungry, of all things the most beautiful; but when you've had your fill, the dregs are disgusting to look at, and you can't wait for someone to take the dish away."

"You're describing a whore, when a man's had too much to drink. Not a lady like Ophelia."

"You might be right," said Hamlet. "I haven't seen her since I came home."

"Hardly seen your uncle, little conversation with your mother, haven't seen Ophelia—they all live here, you know. Do you walk around blindfolded?"

"I haven't sought company," said Hamlet.

"Except the company of books."

"I'm glad you sought me out," said Hamlet. "I didn't know how much I missed you till we talked again."

"And that's how it'll be with Ophelia, I promise you. Whatever love you had for her four years ago will be rekindled when you see her—I promise you, a single look will fan every spark of love into a fire."

"Then why haven't *you* courted her, if the sight of her fans every spark?" asked Hamlet.

Horatio laughed. "Why do you think I'm still in service here, Hamlet? My father's lands won't support my father's family, let alone a son like me at court. I have nothing to offer a lady like Ophelia. I'm the poorest of your Companions."

"The poorest? The best."

"Laertes is and always was the best," said Horatio. "And in case you've forgotten, the best-loved by you."

"Was he?" said Hamlet. "I don't remember."

"It seems to me that memory must have leaked out of your brain to make room for all that logic."

"I never had a favorite," said Hamlet.

"You never showed favor to one over another," said Horatio. "That was the good prince in you. But Laertes could challenge you like no other, and you bore it without anger."

"But I would have borne it from any of you," said Hamlet. "If Laertes was the only one who dared, then that's about him, not me."

"Laertes was the angriest," said Horatio. "I suppose that's all."

"Angriest?" said Hamlet. "What do you mean? At me?"

Horatio blushed. "I meant nothing. He was choleric, that's all. Quick to anger."

But Hamlet knew it was *not* what Horatio meant. There was some grievance, and Horatio meant not to speak of it.

Well, Hamlet wouldn't force the issue. Those days with his Companions were done with now.

They soon made their way out to the practice grounds and Hamlet drew his sword for the first time in years, not because he cared whether he was still good at the art of swordplay, but for old times' sake.

"You have to *try*," said Horatio. "It's no fun to best you when you aren't even trying."

"I *am* trying," said Hamlet. "You're a soldier now, and I'm a scholar."

"Yes, which has nothing to do with how you fight, only with how much or little you care about fighting."

"I'm not angry with you," said Hamlet. "Nor do I mind being defeated by you. I'm dueling for company."

Horatio laughed. "You've become a lunatic! Imagine—a man so lonely that the only way he can have any companionship is to challenge someone to a duel!"

Hamlet laughed with him. "That would be a miserable life! You'd make a friend and have him only long enough to kill him."

But in the next bout, Hamlet began to concentrate on what he was doing, instead of playing around. Only now, when he was actually trying to fight well, remembering some of his old moves, did he begin to see how much better Horatio was than he used to be. Tricks that would have disarmed Horatio back in the old days were now parried skillfully, and Horatio soon pressed on him in a way that Hamlet had never seen from him.

"Now we're playing well together," said Horatio. "Like musicians in tune."

"You've learned a few things," said Hamlet.

"And you've forgotten a few," said Horatio. "But not as many as you think."

Then Horatio made a brute-force move to disarm him, and Hamlet, alert now, side-stepped and spun the sword out of Horatio's hand, all in one quick, dancing move. Horatio's own momentum sent him sprawling into the dirt. He got up laughing. "I should have known!" he said. "You were toying with me!"

"Hardly," said Hamlet. "I'd never seen that move before— no one was strong enough to try anything like that."

"I thought it *might* work."

"It almost did," said Hamlet. "My heart's beating as if I had just swum from Sweden. You gave me a scare!"

"Well, that's something," said Horatio. "But don't give me any more nonsense about how you've forgotten all your skills with the sword."

"Be honest, Horatio. Beating you never took *all* my skills."

"With a *sword,* maybe," said Horatio, smiling with mock malice. "If we stood at either end of a stone wall, pitching heavy rocks as we walked toward each other, I bet I'd win."

"Unless you got confused and threw your head at me."

Whereupon they began a wrestling match, which ended as such matches always did, with Hamlet flat on his back, fully pinned, and Horatio nonchalantly pretending not to see the prince wriggling under him to get free.

Hamlet's Father

At supper they were boisterous enough to draw the attention of King Claudius, but it was a smile he gave them, not a frown. "I'm glad to see your grief at your father's death has eased enough to give you room to laugh," he said.

Grief at Father's death? But Hamlet could hardly say, in front of the whole court, that he barely remembered that he'd *had* a father, and it was only his native soberness of mind and carefulness that he kept him so quiet up to now. "For a moment with an old friend I forgot my grief, sir," said Hamlet. "But at your reminder, the shadow of mourning is reawakened, and I regret it if I seemed to show disrespect to my father's memory."

"I meant no rebuke to you, Prince Hamlet," said Claudius.

"And I did not take it that way," said Hamlet. "I rebuke myself, and thank you for helping me remember my duty to my father."

Hamlet had meant it to be a conciliatory statement, but Mother frowned a little, and the way Claudius turned away to converse with someone on the other side of the table left Hamlet wondering what he had done wrong. The currents in this court were too tricky for him; Aquinas was plain and simple compared to the moods of kings and queens.

Hamlet found himself wishing he could go home. Even though he *was* home, supposedly.

It was the middle of the night two days later when Hamlet awoke from a dream of being awakened in a monastic cell to join his holy brothers for prayers. It was no monk shaking him, though—it was Horatio.

"Hamlet," he said. "Quietly, quietly...nothing's wrong, except I need you to come with me."

"It's full dark outside," said Hamlet.

"Last night I thought maybe it was too much wine at dinner," said Horatio, "but then in the morning I had no headache, and I realized that I had drunk only a little."

"What are we talking about?" said Hamlet as he dressed.

"I think I saw your father last night."

Hamlet looked at him sharply. "Didn't you hear? He died. Or are you saying that the whole kingdom is deceived and he's only pretending to be dead?"

"Dead," said Horatio. "I saw him dead, but walking the battlements of the castle."

"A ghost," said Hamlet, not even trying to conceal his skepticism.

"He looked right at me," said Horatio, "but with such contempt that…I don't think I'm the one he wanted to see."

"Spirits are either in heaven or hell," said Hamlet. "They don't walk the earth."

"Excellent," said Horatio. "I'm glad to hear it. In fact, I told the ghost so myself, but he ignored me and continued to exist. Perhaps tonight, if you tell him, he'll go."

Horatio's words were light and bantering, but his voice trembled a little, so Hamlet knew he was frightened. And nothing frightened Horatio.

"Has he been seen tonight?" asked Hamlet as they left his room.

"He came last night in the hour just before dawn, and left when the light came. Marcellus and Bernardo saw him first, and then brought me. Every night he comes."

"And the word of this hasn't already flown through the castle?"

"They're afraid of being thought lunatics," said Horatio.

"But you have no such fear?"

"I don't fear the opinions of fools," said Horatio.

"So you fear only the ghost itself?"

"No," said Horatio. "A spirit is airy, it's nothing, not even a fog. I could see through it, the walls behind it. When it passed between me and Marcellus, I could see Marcellus plainly. What is there to fear from something insubstantial?"

"And yet you're afraid," said Hamlet.

Horatio was silent until they came to the stair leading up to the battlement. "I'm afraid," said Horatio, "because of what the thing might say."

"Its body isn't real," said Hamlet, "but its words might be?"

"Words can be as sharp as swords, and stab as deep. I fear that what this ghost might have to say will leave this castle draped with corpses."

"Or perhaps he'll have words to save us," said Hamlet. "Perhaps he knows something of the plans of Fortinbras."

"Why should Hell care what befalls kingdoms here above?"

"Hell?" asked Hamlet.

"Or heaven," added Horatio.

"You're sure my father must be in hell?"

Again Horatio kept his silence.

Marcellus and Bernardo waited, sitting and leaning in a corner. "If I didn't know better," said Hamlet, by way of greeting, "I'd say that you were drunk."

"I wish we were, Your Highness," said Bernardo.

"Fellow soldiers now," said Hamlet. "On guard against the world invisible."

"I wish it *were* invisible," said Marcellus.

"We'll be glad of it someday," said Horatio with bravado. "To tell our grandchildren that we saw the ghost of the old King on the battlements in the days before he was buried."

"No doubt that's why he appears to you," said Hamlet. "Because his body has been so long kept out of the tomb."

"Then in God's holy name," whispered Bernardo, "let's bury him."

"Deep," said Marcellus.

"When should we expect him?"

"Soon," said Horatio. "The same time every night—he walks for half an hour, and leaves at the first light in the east."

"Nonsense," said Hamlet, trying to lighten the mood. "My father would never flee from anything he saw coming from Sweden."

They didn't laugh. Instead, Marcellus turned his face away and pointed at something behind Hamlet.

Hamlet turned, and there he was, staring coldly at him: His father, just as he was in life, except insubstantial, like a few wisps of fog so clearly defined that Hamlet could see his features, the expression on his face, and above all, his eyes, which shone as if black fire burned within them.

"Father," he whispered.

The ghost said nothing, but looked at Hamlet and did not move.

"Have you come to give us warning?" asked Hamlet. "To protect the kingdom?"

"He never speaks," whispered Bernardo. "We've asked him all these questions.

"I'm not the king, Father," said Hamlet. "Should I bring your brother Claudius here to confer with you?"

The ghost's face shivered and contorted as if a hot wind had come to melt it or blow it away.

"No," it said.

Bernardo cried out in alarm, and Marcellus whimpered. Hamlet did not blame them. It was not a human voice; it seemed not to fall upon his ears, but struck in his heart, shaking his heart like the tones of a deep bell rung loud and close.

"Are you my father?" asked Hamlet. "Or some demon in disguise?"

"If he means to deceive you," murmured Horatio, "then he'll give the same answer as any honest spirit."

Hamlet's Father

Still the ghost did not take his gaze from Hamlet. "He wants to talk to me," said Hamlet. "Now that we know he's capable of speech, leave us alone so I can hear his message."

"I won't leave you," said Horatio. "What if it means to harm you?"

"Why would my father want to hurt me?" asked Hamlet. Though he recognized the question as soon as he asked it—it was the very one he had asked inside his heart through all the years of growing up without ever having his father's high regard or company.

"A ghost may not be able to strike you," said Horatio, "but what if he entices you off the battlements, to fall to your death?"

"Then either I'll be deceived, and die, or not, and live," said Hamlet. "But you can see this spirit is not to be denied. Let me speak alone with him, or he'll be back again and again."

"I don't want to leave you," said Horatio. "This is our watch of the night."

"You would stand with me before any mortal foe," said Hamlet. "No one doubts your courage or your loyalty. Nor would you abandon your post. But this is a spirit, and no man has any strength against it. As Prince I order you to go, then, and leave me to hear his message."

It took no more words, but several minutes yet for Horatio to get Bernardo onto his feet and Marcellus with him, and shepherd them down from the battlements.

"Why have you come here, Father?" asked Hamlet.

The lips did not move, and yet it spoke. "Avenge me," he said.

More than the sight of the ghost itself, more than the way its words shook his body, the idea that his father had been murdered struck him hard and deep. For he knew at once that there was only one man who might have done it—the man who now wore the crown in Father's place.

The brother whom Father had mistreated from childhood; the brother who had won the respect of the barons; the brother that all were glad to follow, now that Fortinbras of Norway was threatening war.

The uncle Hamlet loved more than he ever loved his father.

"So you came with no message to benefit the kingdom?" asked Hamlet.

Rage came to his father's face then, and he loomed closer. And yet the closer he came, the more transparent he was to Hamlet's eyes, so he could barely see his father's spirit.

The words, though, rung more harshly with the ghost almost on top of him. "Murder and usurpation, treason and adultery," said the ghost. "I live now in Hell. Will you have all Denmark join me there? Avenge me, and purify this kingdom."

"Who killed you, Father?"

"You know already," said the ghost. It backed away.

"How was it done?" asked Hamlet.

"Do you doubt me?"

"Will I kill my uncle on the word of one witness?" asked Hamlet.

"No one but the murderer saw the crime!"

"How will it benefit Denmark for me to kill my uncle now, with Fortinbras preparing his long ships against us?"

"I speak of blood and horror in your own family, and you answer me with fleets and armies."

"What duty do I owe to you?" asked Hamlet.

"Then you consent to my death, and God will damn you as a patricide."

"Why should I listen now, who never heard your voice when you were still alive?"

"I was a better father to you than you know," said the ghost.

Hamlet said nothing, trying to think how his father could have been worse.

"I never laid a hand on you," the ghost said.

"Not your hand, not your heart, barely your eyes if you could keep from seeing me."

"My beautiful son," said the ghost.

"Too late," said Hamlet.

"My sweet, pure-hearted, golden-haired, lovely, strong, and clever son. How often I stood at the window and watched you practice with the sword, the grace of God upon you, the sun shining in your hair. You were the only joy in my life."

Hamlet gasped and sank to his knees. To hear these words now...

"The only good gift your mother gave me. My only hope for the future. All lost. All stolen from me just when I was ready to take you into my confidence and set you on the throne beside me."

Is this what Uncle Claudius stole from me? The hope of having, at last, my father's love? "Why did you wait?" whispered Hamlet. "Why did you keep me at such a distance?"

"I would have coddled you. Spoiled you. I needed you to be a man of firm resolve. Strong, cold-blooded as a king must be, and yet I knew I injured you. Even that was a gift to my people: Out of your anguish would come your compassion. A just and merciful judge you would have been, but now you are supplanted, as I was supplanted."

"I'm a scholar now."

"You are the healer of the kingdom's wounds," said the ghost.

"When we have the victory over Fortinbras," said Hamlet.

"There will be no victory," said the ghost. "Not with Denmark led by a murderer and adulterer."

"My mother was hasty to marry your brother," said Hamlet, "but you were dead, and it was not adultery."

"Better my death would have been, if I had left a faithful widow behind me."

"Do you say my mother sinned with him while you were still alive, Father?"

"I knew it in my heart for many years," said the ghost. "Our bed turned cold when you were still a baby. I was content, to think we had this one perfect son, and no other to rival him. But your mother is young. She means to bear more sons. She means to kill me again as my brother slew me first, for he killed my body, but she will kill all my seed. You are doomed, if you do not strike first."

"To avenge a crime I might strike," said Hamlet. "But not to win a throne. I'll take holy orders and go abroad."

"Why do you think that you were born?" demanded the ghost. "To whimper in some monastery? To scratch on parchment all your life? No! To sit the throne and wear the crown and rule this kingdom after me! Avenge me!"

"There was no mark on your body."

"I lay asleep in the garden," said the ghost. "He crept near enough to pour a savage poison into my ear. It burned through into my brain so quickly that I was dead before I could rise up. The heart stopped in my chest so quickly that I never bled. If any other had approached me, I would have woken up, but his footstep had been part of my life since he was born, and in my sleep I felt no fear of him. This is why treason is of all crimes the most detested by heaven. It is an act made possible by love and trust. Nature shudders when such deeds are done. Didn't you feel the earth shake, even there in Heidelberg?"

"I felt nothing," said Hamlet.

"And feel nothing even now," said the ghost contemptuously.

"I feel too much."

"If you love me, avenge me."

"How could I love you? What did you ever give me to love?"

"I gave you life. What more does a father need to give? You were born with the duty of reverence to me. Nothing I did or didn't do absolves you of that duty."

"And you had no duty to me?"

"I fulfilled my duty to you, better than you know."

The second time he'd made that claim. "Tell me now," said Hamlet, "and then it *won't* be better than I know."

"Are you my true son?" asked the ghost. "Your deeds will show."

"I will serve justice," said Hamlet.

"Then you will serve me, for my cause is just."

"I never saw a murderous nature in my Uncle Claudius."

"Do you argue with a spirit bound for Hell? Stay your hand, then. I will walk the earth in agony until my murder is avenged and justice served, but what is that to you? Young as you are, you're content to let the earth fill up with suffering souls, so long as you're not inconvenienced."

"Why should I hurry you on to eternal torment?"

"The torment is here upon the earth," said the ghost. "The torment is knowing that I was murdered, and no one lives who will avenge me. Must I choose another to be my son? Must I lay this charge on one of your Companions? Then they are my sons in truth."

"I am your son!" cried Hamlet.

"Then swear to me that you will do what sons do: Avenge me!"

"I swear it," said Hamlet.

"And will you keep your word?"

"I swear by God. I swear in the name of Christ. May my own heart be torn out if I do not serve justice in this matter."

"Do it, and we will not meet again until you die."

"You will be at rest soon enough, then, Father," said Hamlet.

But even before he finished the sentence, the ghost was gone. Hamlet looked only at the stones of the battlement.

I have sworn to kill my father's murderer. To do justice. But how can I be sure that justice would be served by killing Claudius? He is my mother's husband now, which should be a cause of mercy, unless he and she were adulterers together before my father's death. And I always loved him better than my own father—should I kill him now, for causing a death I did not grieve for?

Yes, if he killed my father. But that's the question, isn't it? As the ghost said, Only the murderer was witness to the deed. Not my father—he was asleep. Are ghosts so quickly made, that they can see, in the moment of the body's dying, how it died, and at whose hand?

He called me beautiful. He watched me from the window as I practiced with my sword. He wanted me to have his throne.

Or does he only know that these are the words to make me serve him as his slave? Am I his puppet, killing where he wants murder done? He says he's already tied to Hell. What more can he suffer, then, for the sin of lying to me? What if he only wants to bring down his brother?

What kind of man *was* my father? For that's the kind of man he must be now. Souls don't change their nature, merely because the body's set aside. If he had a lying nature then, he'll lie now, too. If he was spiteful then, he'll claim vengeance where none is owed him.

This much is sure: The spirits of the righteous do not walk the earth. They are caught up into heaven, and look no more upon this poor land of shadows, having beheld the light that can be seen only by the pure in heart. My father is here because he was a wicked man. Now he is an angry spirit, and mine are the hands that he has chosen to act out his rage.

And yet by justice and ancient law, my hands *do* belong to him, until his murder be avenged.

Horatio and the others were waiting at the bottom of the stair.

"Go up," said Hamlet. "Resume your watch. He'll never come again, or if he does, it's just to speak to me, and all you need to do is fetch me here at once. But swear to me now that you won't speak of this to anyone."

"I swore as much before you asked," said Bernardo. "Do you think I want my friends to think I'm a superstitious fool? But I swear again, a solemn oath."

"I swear it too," said Marcellus. "No man will know of any spirits walking here, tonight or any other night."

"And you, Horatio?" said Hamlet.

"Do you need any more oath," he said, "than my vow of loyalty and obedience from when we both were lads? Then you have my oath all over again. No one will learn from me of anything you tell me to keep to myself."

"You have always been worthy of my trust," said Hamlet. "I know you still are. So you, Marcellus, Bernardo, is it still your watch?"

"Till dawn," said Marcellus.

"Then go up and keep watch. Fortinbras might come at any time."

"We will, sir," said Marcellus.

At once they jogged up the stairs, leaving Hamlet and Horatio by themselves.

"What did he want to say?" asked Horatio.

"Good-bye," said Hamlet.

"Where are you going?"

"He wanted to tell his son good-bye," said Hamlet. "I'm not going anywhere."

Horatio laughed nervously.

"What passed between my father and me is for us alone," said Hamlet. "For him to say, and for me to remember."

"I'll never ask again, my prince," said Horatio.

"Even if I choose not to tell," said Hamlet, "I'll never be offended by the asking."

"Then I'll ask this: Was he murdered? Did he ask you to avenge him?"

"Do *you* believe that someone murdered him?" asked Hamlet.

"It would take a fool not to wonder," said Horatio. "Too many people stood to benefit from his death. It might have been some spy from Fortinbras. It might have been an agent of some Baron."

"But there was no mark on the body," said Hamlet.

Horatio laughed. "I'm only a soldier," he said. "But I always thought assassins must know ways to kill a man that leave no marks upon the body."

"I want to hear more of your suspicions, Horatio," said Hamlet. "Who you think did the deed, and how."

"You've already heard it all, my Prince," said Horatio. "I only wondered if your father's death might have been unnatural. But I couldn't bring myself to suspect those who benefitted most, since one is King, and the other is the mother of my dearest friend."

"You think this is a benefit for her, then?"

Hamlet's Father

"Isn't a younger husband always better for a woman?"

"Faithful love of your husband, that's what's better," said Hamlet. "And I'll kill any man who says my mother wronged my father before he died."

"No one says she did," said Horatio. "But it's hard for some to believe she would have wed so quickly if she hadn't already felt some swelling of affection for your uncle."

"Then I hope such people keep their opinions to themselves, so my sword can stay unstained with such unworthy blood."

Horatio put a hand on Hamlet's shoulder. "I don't believe any story that would have your mother *or* your uncle doing wrong by your father. I believe them both to be honorable. And their quick marriage was, I think, to ensure your place. Doesn't your uncle mean to adopt you as his heir?"

"I haven't spoken to him alone since I got home," said Hamlet. "He seems shy to speak to me."

"For fear you believe the rumors, I'd bet," said Horatio.

"No one has anything to fear of me," said Hamlet. "And yet they all walk around me as carefully as if I were a skittish horse, ready to kick at the first shadow."

"What *did* the ghost say to you? I heard you say, 'I swear.'"

"Then you were listening closer than a loyal friend should have."

"You shouted it, Hamlet. How could I help but hear the words, and wonder what great oath you had taken with a ghost?"

"An oath of filial duty," said Hamlet. "Beyond that I'm sworn not to say, and I'd count it as a kindness if you *didn't* ask, after all. Now walk with me to the garden where my father died. I want to see the place."

"Garden?" asked Horatio.

"He told me he lay sleeping in the garden."

"I didn't know that," said Horatio. "I thought they found him in his bed."

"He said the garden," said Hamlet.

"Then let's go look at it."

IT WAS A private garden, walled off from the rest of the grounds of the castle. From the outside, it looked cold and stony; once Hamlet passed through the doorway, though, he could see why Father had come to the place, had considered it a refuge. The walls were not visible, completely hidden behind greenery. The stones were covered with ivy, and the ivy was hidden behind shrubbery, much of it evergreen. A few stately shade trees offered respite from a summer sun; tall firs blocked the northwest, shielding from the blasts of winter; and yet the garden was large enough for flowerbeds to flourish in full sunlight.

It was among the flowers that two stone benches were arranged so that two might sit on each bench, across from each other in earnest conversation; or one might lie down on a single bench. A tall man, like Father, could not lie on his back without his legs dangling; but he could curl up on his side, his knees bent, his head pillowed on one arm, and nap in the sunlight on a day in spring.

And someone could creep up behind him and pour cold poison into his ear, first to chill his skin and then to burn its way into his brain.

Did he waken at the cold touch of the poison? Waken, and try to rise? What if the killer held him down? Covered his mouth until the poison had done its work? Hamlet tried to picture what the murderer had seen. He must have been fearful of being discovered. He must have planned what to do or say if Father was awake. He must have had a legitimate errand. Yet it could not have been a decision of the moment—the murderer had to be hoping the King would be asleep, and brought the poison in the expectation of using it.

Hamlet turned and looked upward toward the battlements of the castle itself. It loomed to the northeast of the garden, where it would never cast shade.

But between the castle and the garden a row of pines had been planted. All year they would thickly block any view of what took place in the garden, except at the northwest and southeast corners. The garden was a place for privacy. Once inside these walls, a man could do what he wanted without fear of being seen, unless he was careless.

"What are you looking at?" asked Horatio.

"There's no view of this place from the battlements."

"He didn't come here for company," said Horatio.

"And yet he *had* company," said Hamlet.

"Once too often, I suppose, if this is where it was done."

"If it was done," said Hamlet.

"Do you doubt his word?"

"I haven't told you what his words were," said Hamlet. "Nor shall I. So I can hardly tell you my doubts, or if I have any."

"Then you have no need of me here," said Horatio.

"More need than you know," said Hamlet. "Because you knew him."

"Who?"

"My father. Who else?"

"I feared that you thought I knew his murderer."

"If you did, you would have told it," said Hamlet. "You knew my father, as I could not."

"If anyone knew him," said Horatio.

"Everyone knew him better than I did," said Hamlet. "Why would a man come to a garden to sleep on a hard bench, when he has a dozen soft beds he could sleep in, if he chose?"

"A king is a warrior. Perhaps he hardened himself for war."

"The way a monk punishes himself, to get ready for the fires of Hell?"

"I thought they did it to avoid those fires," said Horatio, chuckling.

"It depends on the monk," said Hamlet.

"I think it likely," said Horatio, "that your father slept in the garden when he wearied himself with working here."

"Working?"

Horatio looked embarrassed. "Working here," he said. "Gardening."

"My father? Gardening?"

"He pruned and planted here. It was spring. My guess is that he lay down in the warm sun after planting those flowers that are already blooming now."

"My father, with his own hands?"

"He kept a pair of shears, a hook, a knife, a saw, and several spades. I thought you knew. This garden was only worked by him, except for carrying away the winterfallen twigs and dead plants. What had died was not for him, but what was alive, that he loved and cared for."

It struck Hamlet with new bitterness. He had more love for plants than for his son.

"This wasn't a secret, surely," said Hamlet.

"Everybody knew. It was how he stilled his mind. After councils, after judgment, he'd come out here. No one disturbed him."

"Yet no one told me," said Hamlet.

"Perhaps," said Horatio, "it did not occur to anyone that you might not know."

"Then someone would have said in passing, Oh, Prince Hamlet, when your father comes in from the garden, or Oh, Prince Hamlet, have you seen the fine work your father has done with that old hedge?"

Horatio looked away.

"Everyone knew that I was not to be spoken to about my father."

"It seemed to cause you pain," said Horatio. "No one wanted to hurt you."

Hamlet sighed. "I wish I were back in Heidelberg."

"You've spoken to your father now," said Horatio. "He came to talk to you, even after death. Hell could not stop him."

"Nor heaven," said Hamlet.

"I imagine God *could* have stopped him, but chose not to."

"A spirit comes to me," said Hamlet. "Does that mean it has God's consent to come? Are its words therefore the words that God intends for me to hear?"

"Did the spirit of Samuel come to Saul through the witch of Endor by God's consent?" asked Horatio. "Or does Hell send its angels to further the cause of evil in the world?"

"So you've studied the Old Testament," said Hamlet. "And philosophy."

"I was tutored by a priest who loved to terrify us with ghost stories."

"Spirits of the dead with messages for the living. Do they ever come with good news?"

"Did this one?" asked Horatio.

"No," said Hamlet.

"I wonder," said Horatio, "on which of these benches your father lay when he was slain."

"I wonder," said Hamlet, "who was the slayer?"

Horatio looked up at him heavy-lidded eyes. "*Do* you wonder, my prince?" he asked.

Hamlet shook his head. "No," he said. "My father told me who it was."

"And you don't believe him?"

Hamlet didn't know how to answer. He believed—of course he did. And yet, despite his oath, he felt a terrible dread at the thought of acting on that belief. "I believe and don't believe," he said.

"Why? Do spirits lie?" asked Horatio.

"Spirits from Hell might deceive," said Hamlet.

"Then Spirits from Hell will *say* they came from heaven," said Horatio, "so how can we know which ones to trust?"

Father did not pretend to come from heaven. "Spirits from Hell might sometimes lie and sometimes not."

"What will you do, if you become certain?" asked Horatio.

Hamlet looked away at the flowers. Bees alit and rose again from the blooms, yellowed with pollen. How quickly the flowers must have bloomed, if Father only recently planted them. If you asked me, from the evidence of my eyes, how long these plants had been in place, I would have said a month at least. Yet I believe Horatio because he's a truthful friend, and because he has no reason to lie. Was that faith? Knowledge? Probability? Mere desire to believe?

"Certainty is a hard thing to achieve," said Horatio.

"If to know a thing is to feel certain of it, then most people achieve it all the time, especially about the things they think about least. But if to know a thing is to be certain *and* be right, and *know* that you're right, then that's another matter."

"Certainty is about how you feel," said Horatio, nodding. "But being right is about what truly happened in the past. What you feel means nothing."

"That's a good thing," said Hamlet, "since I feel no certainty."

"And yet you swore an oath."

"I can be certain of what *I* will do, even when I'm not certain of what others have done."

Horatio smiled grimly. "But can you be certain of the rightness of the act?"

"Some acts are always right," said Hamlet. "And some are always wrong."

"You learned more in Heidelberg than I thought was possible," said Horatio. "If they told you which was which."

"I'm not sure where I learned it, except that I know it's true."

"In other words," said Horatio, "you *feel* certain that it's true."

"Something has to be sure in this world," said Hamlet.

"Why?" asked Horatio.

"Because if we could never be sure, we'd never be able to act. No man would ever marry a woman, no soldier would ever fight for his king and his country, no tailor would ever cut his cloth, and no man of trade would ever trust the value of the money he was paid."

"As long as we're talking philosophy," said Horatio, "then just because people have to believe in something enough to act on it doesn't mean that they're right, not ever."

"Then we live like animals in this world, not knowing right from wrong."

"Muddling through," said Horatio.

"And God judges us for *that*?" asked Hamlet.

"Let God judge as he judges. Let *us* remember that we don't have God's knowledge."

"Amen," said Hamlet.

Horatio rose to his feet, agitated. He moved away from Hamlet, then came back. "I don't believe you believe what you said, my prince. That some things are always right or always wrong."

"I do believe it," said Hamlet.

"What if one of Herod's men, hearing the command to slay all the innocent babes of Bethlehem, had decided instead that he would strike down the giver of that command rather than obey it? It's always wrong to kill innocent babies, isn't it? Even if your king commands? And it's always wrong to kill the king, isn't it? Even if he means to do something evil?"

"Are you sure you didn't sneak off to some university yourself?" said Hamlet.

"You don't need a professor to wrestle with the hard questions," said Horatio. "And you wrote me letters."

"Not about this."

"You told me what the great questions were. And your father let me read his books."

"Father read books?" asked Hamlet.

"The testaments only," said Horatio. "But I have Latin enough for that."

"So all your philosophy comes from scripture."

"You didn't answer me about Herod's good soldier."

"Why must he choose between murderous treason and murderous obedience? Why not run away?"

"Like Jonah?" said Horatio. "If you know that King Herod's vile order will be obeyed by someone, and you run away when you could have prevented the slaughter of the innocents, then how are you any less guilty than the ones who wield the swords?"

"But if you kill Herod, you'll die. They'll torture you to death as a traitor."

"There are worse things than death, my prince."

"Are there?" asked Hamlet.

"Of all men, you should be most certain of that," said Horatio.

"Why?"

"Other men fear death because they don't know if the soul survives. But you've spoken to your father. You know the ghost was real because I and two other witnesses also saw him. Why would *you* fear death now? Or me? Knowing that life continues."

"It's the continuation of life," said Hamlet, "that might be the most fearful thing. Maybe death would hold less fear if we knew it *was* the end of all."

"Is this what you pondered all those times you went to the graveyard alone?" asked Horatio.

"What this garden was to my father," said Hamlet, "the cemetery was to me."

"A place to nap?"

"A place to listen to my own soul."

"My prince," said Horatio, "you know that whatever you decide is right, I will be your true friend and loyal servant."

"You're not my Companion anymore, my friend, and your duty is to your King, not to a prince who will never ascend a throne."

"You don't know you'll have no throne," said Horatio.

"I would refuse it if it was offered me. That's how I know. But it will never be offered."

"Then your resolve will die untested," said Horatio.

Hamlet laughed. "My whole life is one long round of preparing for a test I'll never face. To be king, but now I'll be no king. To be a good son to my father, but while he lived he never gave me the chance to try. As a child I dreamed of greatness. I practiced for war. I practiced for government. At the university I even practiced for holy orders. But I'll never govern, never go to war, and never take orders either."

"You might," said Horatio.

Hamlet did not say, they rarely ordain a man during the few hours between murdering a king and being drawn and quartered for the crime. He merely looked away.

"God doesn't judge us by whether men think we're great or not," said Horatio.

"No, his standard is even harsher. It's easier to be great than to be good, and easier to be good than to do right."

"There's a distinction there too fine for me to see."

"A good man does what he believes is right. He might be wrong about what's right, but because he intended to do good, he's a good man."

Horatio nodded gravely. "Whatever you swore to your father, Hamlet, don't be afraid to do it."

Am I afraid? "I'm not."

"Don't hesitate," said Horatio.

Trust a man who never trusted me. Strike down an uncle I have always loved, for the sake of a father who never loved me. Why would I hesitate to do that? "I won't," said Hamlet.

"And yet you stay your hand."

If I strode into King Claudius's court with drawn sword, I would be dead before I got near enough to strike. "God has not yet put the opportunity before me," said Hamlet. Some secrets are too heavy for a man to want to burden his friends.

Besides, Horatio had already made his point, with that story of Herod: If he knew that Hamlet meant to kill the king, Horatio would have no choice but to kill Hamlet first. You do wrong to prevent a greater wrong; thus wrong becomes right.

DID MARCELLUS AND Bernardo keep their word, and tell no one of the ghost? Hamlet couldn't help but wonder; wherever he went in the castle, on the grounds, in the stables, anywhere at all, he could feel all eyes upon him. They may not know the charge that his father had placed upon him by oath, but they seemed to have heard that a ghost had visited him; they looked at him as one with a fey upon him, a mixture of dread and pity.

And if word had spread of a ghost, then surely they had guessed whose ghost it was; and if they knew who it was, then it took no scholar to guess what the ghost had sworn Hamlet to do.

If King Claudius was, indeed, a bloody-handed fratricide, then what would stop him from killing the nephew as easily as he had killed the brother? Then what would come of Hamlet's vengeance, if he himself were dead?

Hamlet's Father

If they look at me as a fey spirit, then let them see what they look for. Let it not be vengeance they see in my eyes, but madness. Let them see an orphan who grieves too much, not a son who calculates revenge. Let me stay alive until I have a chance to get Uncle Claudius alone.

He began his masquerade when by chance he heard laughter up a stair. He thought he knew the voice, and when he bounded up the long flight of steps he soon learned that he was right. It was Ophelia, laughing with one of her maids. Ophelia, who was Laertes' sister and Polonius's daughter, had been only thirteen when Hamlet left for Heidelberg. Even then, he had felt her eyes upon him and had known that, quite apart from any wish of her father that his daughter be allied with the royal house, she herself had thoughts of, if not feelings for, the crown prince of Denmark.

Not any more, thought Hamlet. No crown prince now, and so no dynastic alliance and no yearnings.

But he could make use of her all the same.

He paused for only a moment in the corridor, to half undress himself, as if he had been in the midst of putting on his clothes, but got distracted. Carrying his shoes and doublet, he strode into her room. At once the maid fell silent in the midst of some tale, and Ophelia leapt to her feet, her sewing dropping from its place on her lap to the floor. "Your Highness," she said. "What brings you to my room?"

Hamlet fixed his gaze on her and never let it wander as he walked closer and took her by the hand. She smiled tentatively. He did not smile back; he only stared into her eyes.

"Will Your Highness take refreshment?" she asked.

He said nothing.

"How can I serve you, my lord?" she asked.

Hamlet reached his hand to his forehead and bent over her, almost as if to kiss her. He could hear her breathing more heavily, and saw her close her eyes. For a moment he thought that he had frightened her, that she was about to faint. But then he realized that her lips were parted. She was waiting for a kiss.

That was not what he had intended. She was not supposed to want him now. She had been a sweet girl, when he knew her years ago; she was a pretty woman now, and though he had no particular desire for any of her tribe, he knew it was wrong to trifle with her. She thought he meant something by coming here.

And yet her misunderstanding would do as well as any other purpose. Let them think he was pining for love of her.

But he could not kiss her. That would be a kind of promise, and knowing that soon enough he would be a murderer and traitor, doomed to die, how could he encourage her to love him?

He sighed at his own foolishness. Then sighed again, this time as if in pain. He screwed up his face as if in agony, then fled the room and ran pell-mell along the corridor and down the stairs.

After that he shunned everyone's company for the rest of the day, refusing to let the servants open his door. Whenever he heard footsteps approach, he groaned as piteously as he could. When someone called through the door, "Your Highness, are you well? Are you ill? May I bring you something?" he answered with a muttered "Leave me alone" or "Why are you cursing me like this?" or "What harm have I done you?" Meanwhile, he lay on his bed and read the Confessions of St. Augustine. Here was a miracle and also madness, that the words of a man who lived in Africa before the heathen Arabs stole the land from Christ could speak so powerfully to him now; a man of the south, teaching a man of the north; a priest full of power comforting a prince full of death.

He knew enough of court and courtiers that his absence from dinner would be noticed by everyone; that Ophelia would have gone to her father and her father to the King and Queen;

that they would be guessing about what was going on in Hamlet's mind. If they knew about the ghost, they might think the spirit had driven him mad. If they suspected him of harboring ill will because his uncle had the throne *and* his mother, then they would see him, not as a resolved and dangerous enemy, but as a pouting boy. If they thought he yearned for the love of Ophelia, then perhaps they would be contemplating some kind of wedding. If they thought he was transported by grief for his father's death, they would be thinking of amusements to distract him.

Just so they didn't think to take away his sword, or keep him from the presence of the king. He could seem mad, but not so mad that they would find a need to shut him up behind a locked door, where only the ghost of his father could visit him, to condemn him for having failed so thoroughly.

If they saw him sane, they would be wary of him; if too mad, they would be afraid for another reason; he must hew to the middle ground, so they would leave him to wander about as he wanted, ignoring him or coddling him.

And so it was the next day. It began when he found Rosencrantz and Guildenstern outside his door, waiting on two chairs that hadn't been there earlier. They pretended they had only happened to be there, but were delighted to see him.

It was a simple matter to call them by the wrong names, and then speak of Father as if he were still alive. "Did you mean to join my father on the hunt today?" he asked. "My father goes a-hunting—don't you hear the horns?"

Rosencrantz shied away at this, but Guildenstern only smiled. "The pleasures of the hunt are not done, just because your father is no longer here to enjoy them."

"I hunt like a fisherman," said Hamlet. "I sit in my boat, pull up the net, and see what has come to me."

"Then you'll catch no deer, not in any woods I know of," said Rosencrantz.

"I'll have the eight-pronged buck," Hamlet retorted. "I'll have him through and through with a syllogism—old stags aren't much for logic, it stuns them and they stand there waiting for the dogs."

"What are you talking about, Your Highness?" asked Guildenstern.

"Into your ears, but above your head."

"Let us go with you," said Rosencrantz. "Where are you going?"

"Only a few steps," said Hamlet. "All the way to Hell. No, stay here, there's not room for you yet, I have to sweep out the room where Judas used to dwell. Stay. I don't need you with me right now."

They didn't know what to make of his reference to Judas Iscariot's room in Hell. They would wonder if he was accusing them of disloyalty. Which, of course, he was, since they had obviously been brought to court to try to bring him to his senses.

It was almost fun, and certainly exhilarating, to feign a bit of madness and watch them all hop. Hamlet hadn't realized before how much of his life had been devoted to doing what they all expected of him, acting out the role of prince. Now he had no role, and was improvising a new one that made no one comfortable—except himself. Madness kept them all at a greater distance than his rank had ever done.

Hamlet came into the court with a book in front of his nose; he held it too close to read the letters. Everyone fell silent—Uncle Claudius was hearing someone's petition. Mother rose to her feet as if to go to Hamlet, but Polonius waved her off with a small gesture and took Hamlet by his arm, leading him back out of the room.

"What are you reading?" Polonius asked.

"Words, words, words," said Hamlet.

"And what's the subject?"

"Lesser than the king, but still not nothing."

Hamlet's Father

It took Polonius a moment to realize he had answered another meaning of "subject." "I mean what do you read about?"

"All in a line, back and forth," said Hamlet. "I go from left to right with my mind full, and then must drop it there and head back empty-headed to the left side again, and take up another load to carry forward. It's a most tedious job, and when I'm done, there are all the letters where I found them, unchanged despite my having carried them all into my head."

Polonius laughed, as if he hoped that Hamlet was joking. "As fine a description of reading as I ever heard. But what does the book *say*?"

Hamlet looked at him with pity. "It says that old men grow confused, and ask young men for wisdom. You could listen at this book all day and night and hear nothing, but if you threw it at my head, I'd learn much and you'd hear more."

Polonius looked at him quizzically. "I think you mean something by this."

"More than you think, and less than I know," said Hamlet. "You have a daughter, sir?"

"I have." Polonius's eyes lit up at that. It made Hamlet sad that even a madman would be regarded as an interesting match for his daughter, even if he could only sire mad children on her.

"Be sure to keep her out of the sun," said Hamlet. "Bright sunlight can breed maggots in a dead dog; who knows what it can do to daughters, sir."

"I thank you for your counsel," said Polonius.

"I'm sure it's worth as much as the counsel you gave my mother, sir," said Hamlet. He turned to leave.

"What do you mean by that?" demanded Polonius, following him.

"By what?"

"The counsel I gave your mother. What counsel was that?"

"How should I know what counsel you gave her? I only hoped that mine was as valuable."

"But when?" asked Polonius.

"When you were counseling with her. Must I tell you *all* your business?" Then Hamlet took off at a run.

He felt giddy as he fairly flew down the corridors, watching servants and courtiers shy out of his way. It was a foolish kind of bravery, though, to lie so much that he could then tell the truth and pretend it was also a lie. But dangerous also, for Polonius kept trying to make sense of what he was saying, and there was sense to be made of it, if he only kept at it.

Thus passed the next few days, with Hamlet making forays out of his room, stirring up trouble while seeming innocent.

What he could not determine to his own satisfaction was what he was actually trying to do. Was he really trying to protect himself from suspicion? Or to keep Claudius from fearing him as a rival? Was he biding his time, as he told himself, until he could get his uncle alone and kill him without interference? Or was he doing all this mummery to fill the time and make more and more delay because he hadn't the heart or stomach for murder after all?

More likely he was doing this, he realized, to protect himself. I will do foul treason, but men will not call me a traitor if they think me mad. I will still be slain, but not seen with horror. It will be pity that fills men's hearts when they see my grave or hear my name. Is that what this sham is for, to make my name a sad one instead of an evil one, after I'm dead?

What does it matter? Why should I care?

I'm a coward, that's what my madness is about, to delay the day of action, and then delay some more.

And yet he could not let go of it. They brought Ophelia to him, and now he saw that she was indeed sincere; she spoke to him of how she had thought of him often when he was in

Heidelberg, and waited eagerly for his return, and missed him even more than she missed her brother, who was off in France. It broke his heart, and he regretted his foolish play on the first day of his mad charade. He should not have gone to her.

He could correct it now, though. He could, in the midst of his madness, make sure she understood that she shouldn't look for anything from him. Not love—there was no room for love in a heart that he was trying to steel for murder.

He could have loved her, though, he saw that. If he had come home from Heidelberg without his father dead, without his mother married to his uncle, without a ghost demanding vengeance, then he might have seen this girl and wanted her. He might have courted her with poetry, with pleasantries, with flowers and little gifts, with kisses that were freely given, but pretended to be stolen.

He might have married her, and lain with her, and fathered sons and daughters, not just one as his mother had, but many, and watched Ophelia grow fat with babies and then sat with her to see the children playing in the garden or the fields. They would have taken them out to sea, plying the coasts of Denmark in the long ships that once struck terror throughout the world, but now were meant for wealthy families on pleasure cruises.

It made him angry, to think of what had been taken from him. His father had stolen his childhood, and now was stealing his future as well.

What right do you have, Father? Stay dead. Don't walk the earth swearing your son to loyalty you never showed him when you were alive.

I refuse to kill for you. Does that make me an oathbreaker? To slay a king must be at least as great a sin as breaking an oath. But what about killing a king who is also a murderer himself? Then again, what about breaking an oath to a man who never acted the father to me, yet now expects me to be a true son to him? Where is the justice in any of this? Why does my duty demand that I do the worst thing, or be condemned? To save myself from condemnation, will I damn myself? Am I merely choosing between two different rooms in Hell?

HE WAS SUMMONED on an afternoon when court was finished, and brought without his sword before King Claudius. The soldier—there was only one, a man he did not know—made no special point of coming without a sword. He found Hamlet reading, and urged him to come quickly, so there was no time to arm himself or even dress properly for an audience.

Mother was there, and smiling at him, so it would not be something harsh. Polonius beamed at him also—prospective father-in-law to a madman—but King Claudius looked serious.

"I knew you all your life as my nephew and my prince," said Claudius. "Now, married to your mother, I hope I may also view you as my son. Certainly you are my heir."

"The barons name the king, Your Majesty," said Hamlet. "But I am grateful for your trust in me."

"Here is how far my trust goes. The Orkney Islands have forgotten their duty, or else some terrible storm has destroyed their crop or sunk their fleet. I must send a man I trust, and one whose presence will prove to them my great concern. That man is you, if you will go in my name."

"Like any other Dane, Your Majesty, I will serve you where you ask, honored to be remembered."

"And so that you will not have to do this work unsupported, take Rosencrantz and Guildenstern with you."

So he was *not* trusted. "I'll be grateful for their company," he said.

"Then that's done," said King Claudius.

"Will you have me go at once? Or may I stay until my father's body is laid inside the tomb?"

Uncle Claudius frowned. "Your father's body lies in state; we have not dishonored his memory."

"And yet his burial is delayed. Who knows what unrest this might cause his spirit?" asked Hamlet.

Mother reached over and touched her new husband on the arm.

He did not look at her, but he nodded. "We wait for Polonius's son, Laertes. You know that your father and he were close."

"Closer than he ever was with me," said Hamlet. *But it was I, not Laertes, that he charged to avenge him.* "What will you do, then, Your Majesty? Send away the old King's son before the funeral, and yet await the son of your chancellor?"

Claudius looked stung. "I meant no such insult to my brother's honor or to his son. Of course you can wait to leave for the Orkneys until Laertes comes."

"He's looked for every day," said Mother.

"So I also will look for him." Hamlet knelt a second time before King Claudius. "Your Majesty, may I ask to see my father's body?"

"No," said Claudius.

"May a son not bid good-bye to his father?"

"We keep the corpse on ice," said Claudius. "The days grow warm. We'll keep the icehouse tightly closed until the funeral day."

"The nights are still cool enough. I'll go to him at night."

"And take a lantern's heat into the room? No."

"A single candle," said Hamlet. "Not even that, if you prefer. I can find my father in the dark. I'm not afraid of him." *Though of course he was.*

"Is this another part of your madness?" asked Claudius sharply.

"What madness, Your Majesty?" asked Hamlet.

"The way you spoke to my daughter," said Polonius. "And to Rosencrantz and Guildenstern. And to me!"

"If I said something I should not have said, then I'm ashamed, and heartily beg your pardon."

"The icehouse will not be opened," said Claudius.

"Then open the ancestral tomb and let me in," said Hamlet, "so I can see where my father's body will lie."

"Hamlet," said Mother, "that's morbid."

"No, Mother," said Hamlet. "It's lunatic. I mean to play at juggling with my ancestors' skulls."

She looked as if he had slapped her.

"Do my mother and my uncle mean to keep me from anything that has to do with my father? I last saw him alive four years ago. I look around this court, searching for some sign of grief for him, and I see none."

"There was much grieving before you came home," said King Claudius.

"I came home quickly, and yet the grief was so far done with that I found my widowed mother already married, and a new king on a throne whose previous occupant was still unburied."

"We did as the barons wanted," said Claudius. "Fortinbras is coming."

"I do not argue with the barons' choice," said Hamlet. "I was not ready to lead Denmark's ships and soldiers, and they must be led. You know you have my love and loyalty in all things, Your Majesty. But I am also a son, not only a loyal prince, and I owe a duty to my father. Will you shame me by forbidding me to have any access to the poor remnant his spirit left behind him when he died, or even to the stone house where it will desiccate?"

"The tomb will be unlocked for you," said King Claudius.

"Pardon me, but I would rather have the key, so I can come and go as I wish."

Hamlet's Father

"Then have it," said Claudius. He waved a hand at Polonius. "See to it."

"I thank Your Majesty with all my heart," said Hamlet.

"Please," said Mother. "Come and see me today. You've been home for more than a week, and you haven't come to see me."

"I was not invited until now," said Hamlet. "Of course I'll come. Give me an hour in my father's tomb."

It took more than a little argument to get Rosencrantz and Guildenstern to let him visit the tomb alone. It was obvious they had been assigned to stay with him whenever he ventured out of the walls of the castle. But they had been his Companions, and they knew that when he entered the graveyard he must be alone.

The tomb's lock was ancient but well oiled; it opened readily. The door also opened silently. The house of the royal dead was well tended.

Not so their bodies. The moist sea air could not be kept out, however tightly sealed the tomb might be. The place was damp inside, and the bodies that still had flesh on them sagged onto their stone beds, their fine robes sliding into ragged patches. It looked as if this were some great oven, and the corpses all were melting like butter. The freshest body here was Father's mother, whom Hamlet had known when he was little; she was a nightmare of decay, if Hamlet had not already seen the spirit of her son. Corpses that had no power of speech, that could not lay dire oaths upon him, could not frighten him. What children imagined, terrifying themselves in the dark of night, Hamlet had seen with his own eyes, and lived.

There was no place prepared for Father. No new bed of stone. Did they plan to toss his body on the floor?

Or did they have some plan to bury him at sea, on a flaming ship, like the Viking kings of an earlier time?

It was not about keeping the body cold. It was not about waiting for Laertes. King Claudius did not want his brother's body seen.

There must be some mark on the corpse after all. Some proof that he was murdered. There could be no other explanation for this. He would never lie here in the tomb. Whatever Claudius and Mother might have planned, it did not include putting Father's body on public display.

Hamlet came forth out of the tomb and locked it behind him. The dead were safe enough from his intrusions now; would that he had been kept safe from theirs.

The graveyard itself was familiar ground. What was not familiar was Horatio, perched like a gargoyle atop a simple headstone belonging to some loyal family servant.

"They sent you?" asked Hamlet.

"You're a lunatic, and must be closely watched," said Horatio.

"Better you than Rosencrantz and Guildenstern. They're not the friends that I remember."

"Things changed in the four years you were gone. When the Companions were dissolved at your parting, they decided not to dissolve themselves. Living four years together on Guildenstern's estates has made them as fusty and peculiar as an old married couple. I pity the woman who tries to wed her way into that house."

"They're not my friends at all, I think," said Hamlet.

"They serve the King."

"Don't we all."

A new-dug grave lay open only a few steps away from the stone where Horatio perched. "Who's to be buried here?"

"A cousin of the royal house," said Horatio. "The body will arrive in a day or two. They've already had the funeral, it's just a matter of laying it in the ground."

Hamlet's Father

"I wonder if it's someone that I knew."

"It's your family's graveyard," said Horatio. "You knew them all."

Only then did Hamlet look at the name on the stone where Horatio sat. "Yorick," he read aloud. "Yorick's dead!"

"You've been here this long and didn't notice he was gone?"

"But no one wrote to me," said Hamlet. "I assumed he was away. Or living privately, pensioned off. But dead!"

"Not long after you left," said Horatio. "Suddenly, in his sleep."

"He wasn't old enough to die."

"How old is *that*?" asked Horatio. "I think there are tiny graves enough to prove that death knows how to find us all, however old we might not be."

Hamlet laughed bitterly at that, ashamed of the tears that streamed down his cheeks. "I know you're right, Horatio. But Yorick—it's a terrible thing to say, but his death strikes me harder than my father's." And with that, he turned away and sank down to his knees, crossing himself in respect for the old fool. "He spoke the words I might have heard from my father, if I'd *had* a father," he said.

"Oh, you had father enough, I think," said Horatio.

"One father too many, I sometimes thought," said Hamlet, "and yet one too few. I hated you, every one of you, when he took you with him, spent hours with you, and yet never had time for me."

"It was never by our choice," said Horatio.

"I know it," said Hamlet. "But I've always been a lunatic."

"Playing among the graves? No doubt of it—we all knew it. But what's your game now? Sometimes mad and sometimes lucid."

"It's a lunar lunacy. It rises and sets, waxes and wanes."

"And brings the tides along, no doubt."

"Don't blame the tides on me."

"I blame you for nothing," said Horatio. "I'm only sorry for how things turned out for you. Who would have guessed that your father's death would not mean your accession to the throne? Your mother dotes on you—I would have thought she'd rather die than marry the uncle who took your rightful place."

Hamlet knew he should be angry, to hear Horatio criticizing Mother. But it was the simple truth, and no man should be punished for saying it aloud. At least in private. To a friend.

"Everyone finds his own way in the world," said Hamlet. "And does what seems right. Or at least most useful. Or most desirable."

"Most desirable," said Horatio. "They only do what's right if they desire what's right. Or most useful if they desire to be useful. Always it comes down to desire."

"Then all men are equal, the good and the bad," said Hamlet, "since they do no more than follow their desires."

"But wouldn't you rather live in a country governed by those who desire to do good?" said Horatio.

"And haven't you always preferred to be friends with women who desire to do bad?" said Hamlet.

"I want them to do bad, but do it well."

"Where I try to do good, but do it badly."

"Tell me the burden the ghost laid upon you, Hamlet. Let me counsel with you. How can you be bound by an oath to the dead? Think about it—the most solemn of oaths—holy orders, matrimony—those sacraments dissolve at death. All sacraments do, all oaths, death's the end of them. So how can you even call an oath binding when you make it with one who is already dead? It was dissolved before you swore."

Hamlet shook his head. "I've chopped logic with better hypocrites than you," he said. "Your oath as a Companion is dissolved, and yet you still honor it."

Horatio laughed, but Hamlet had hit him square, and he made no more argument.

"I have to see my mother," said Hamlet.

"And I have to look for the mother of my children," said Horatio.

"Do you have someone in mind?"

"As always, I ask for volunteers, and then choose the best."

"Princes aren't so free."

"Princes are as free as they want to be," said Horatio. "Virtue—which *you* desire—is what keeps you chaste."

"I wish that women were as good company as my Companions were," said Hamlet. "Women seem to want so much. The ones I've met—as a man, that is—they're all enticement, but when you let yourself be lured a little closer, you find out that they have all their plans laid out, and want only a fly to wander into the web. The fly is never consulted about how the strands of the web should go, or where it should be placed."

"There'd be a world of hungry spiders if that were how it worked."

"And far too many flies," said Hamlet. "The analogy breaks down. The parable is false. Aesop's animals are not at risk from any fable of mine." He arose from the ground. "I sat upon old Yorick's grave, and felt the grass of it in my hands. That's more funeral than I'll ever get for my father."

"I thought they waited for Laertes."

"They wait forever. I'll never see my father's body."

"You've seen his spirit," said Horatio. "Isn't that more? You've had the walnut; why would you need the shell?"

"I couldn't weep over the ghost—it wouldn't stop talking long enough."

"Will you weep over the body, then?"

"Yes."

"But you often said that you hardly knew him."

"That's what I'll weep for." He threw his arms around Horatio and held him close. "I'll weep for the boys we were, and for the man I'll never be."

Horatio followed him as he walked away. "What's that supposed to mean? The man you'll never be?"

Hamlet had no intention of telling him how soon he expected to die. "I think I would have been a better man if I'd had a father," he said.

"And what if I say not? Did knowing your father make better men of *us*?"

"It might have," said Hamlet. "But you had your own fathers, all of you—I had none."

"You had Yorick. You had your uncle Claudius."

"Horatio, all I meant was, I'll never know what I would have become, if my father had been a father to me. Now leave me, my friend, unless you intend to greet my mother with me."

Horatio laughed then, and let him go.

ON HIS WAY to his mother's chamber, Hamlet passed the chapel. He heard a voice inside—a priest at prayer, no doubt. And yet he knew the voice, and stopped, and stepped inside.

It was King Claudius who knelt at the altar before a statue of bloody-handed Jesus. Hamlet could not hear his words.

Here he is, alone, with no one to see or hear. I have no sword, but I have my dagger. This is the moment I've been waiting for.

But his hand would not move toward the hilt.

If I kill him at his prayers, his shriven soul will go to heaven, he thought.

And mine will not.

Nothing I do will let my soul go to heaven. Let him live and I'm damned. Kill him and I'm damned.

Hamlet's Father

I can't do it secretly. The way he killed my father—I won't do that. When I slay him it will be in the open for all to see, for everyone to hear me tell them why. He killed my father with stealth, so he could steal all that my father had; I want nothing that he has, and so I do not have to hide my deed.

That's my reason for staying my hand.

And the fact that it is not my desire to kill him, or any man. And rank fear.

Cowards strike from hiding; but I strike not at all. What does that make me? More fearful than a coward.

He moved silently out of the chapel and moved on, threading his way to his mother's room.

Mother was not alone. The door to her chamber opened as Hamlet approached, and there stood Laertes.

Hamlet cried out his name, joyfully, and took a step toward him. But Laertes stepped back, and his manner was cold.

"I hear that you've been trifling with my sister," he said.

"I haven't," said Hamlet.

"She needs no lunatics," said Laertes.

"Then she'll have none," said Hamlet. "Laertes, is this our greeting after four years?"

Laertes bowed. "My prince," he said. "You look well."

"And you do *not*," said Hamlet, trying to jolly him into a smile. "You're thin. Don't you eat? You look as if you've sharpened your face."

"I live by the blade now," said Laertes. "Haven't you heard? I'm quite the swordsman now."

"What, have you strewn the fields of France with the bodies of duelists?"

"I've watered them with their blood, though none have died," said Laertes. "So be warned. I'll brook no insult to my sister."

"Are you threatening me?"

"I'm telling you of the consequences. Good day, sir." Laertes pushed past him and was gone.

Hamlet looked after him for a moment, then turned and strode into his mother's chamber. "Why is Laertes so angry with me?"

"He's had a hard four years," said Mother. "But he's home now, and we'll get him right, soon enough."

"If he doesn't kill me first," said Hamlet. "What was my offense?"

"That mad display you put on for Ophelia," said Mother. "You have to tell me now, my son. Was that some attempt to show her how much you love her? Or something else? She's a sweet girl, and worthy of a prince, if you want her to wife; but too good to be trifled with, or teased, or mocked—there are girls in the kitchen that will play those games with you, if that's the sort of man you are."

"You know it's not."

"I know that I don't understand a thing you do or say since you returned."

"Which brings us to a balance, my lady mother."

"We've hardly seen each other," she said.

"I've seen enough of you to know what you've become."

"Have you forgotten the respect you owe me?"

"No more than you've forgotten it yourself," said Hamlet. "Did you have them put my father's corpse on ice so you'd be sure it was cold before you got into my uncle's bed?"

She flung out her hand to slap him, but he caught her by the wrist. "You won't strike me for saying the truth," he said.

"You don't know what's true,' she said.

"I know my father hated me," said Hamlet, "and yet I seem to be the only one in Denmark who ever loved him."

"Don't judge what you don't understand."

"If there's something I don't understand, is that my fault? No one has told me anything my whole life. Did you hate my father? Is that why he hated me?"

"Your father never hated you," said Mother.

"Then why didn't he ever take me with him? I had no part of him."

"Because I forbade it," she said.

"You—why?"

"For good enough reason," she said. "And that's the end of it."

"That's not even the beginning," said Hamlet. "That was nothing—do you think you'll make me love my father better by making me hate you?"

"Your father's dead. It came in good time for Denmark—and for me."

Hamlet seized her by the shoulders and dragged her from her chair. "So you knew! You knew that Uncle Claudius murdered him!"

"Let go of me!"

He threw her down onto the ground. "You don't even deny it."

"Of course I deny it! Your uncle never raised a hand against your father!"

"Who did it, then? You? Poison is a woman's tool—I should have known."

"What are you talking about? No one murdered your father!"

"I know a lie when I hear one. All you're doing is convincing me that you're part of the conspiracy."

He drew his dagger. If Claudius was still in the chapel, he would kill him now, prayer or no prayer. After what he'd said to his mother, there would be no secret about who did it.

But when she saw the dagger, she mistook the prey he intended to kill with it.

"Help! No! Someone help me! He means to kill me!"

And then a second voice, behind a tapestry, crying out, "Stop! Help! To the queen!"

Hamlet whirled to the curtain, saw the hands trying to brush it aside, saw the feet moving blindly forward, and in a moment he had his dagger through the cloth and into the man's chest, whoever it was.

For a moment the man hung heavily upon the blade, supported by the thickness of the tapestry.

The fabric was thick, and held; the blade was strong, and did not break. But the hangings of the tapestry were slender and too few, and they gave way. The tapestry came down, and the man pitched forward. Hamlet pulled his blade away, which turned the body from him; when it fell, he lay upon his back. It was Polonius.

"You killed him!" cried Mother.

"He was hiding in your chamber," said Hamlet. "What was he doing here? Concealed? I thought he was a murderer."

Two soldiers appeared in the doorway. One of them was Marcellus. "What happened here?"

"I saw a man was hiding behind the tapestry. Mother called for help. I slew him through the cloth. I didn't see his face until he fell."

He did not turn to look at Mother. Everything he said was true; it was up to her if she wanted to correct what he said and tell them that it was her son she feared, and not the hidden observer.

For that was what he surely was. Polonius must have been meeting with Mother and Laertes, and when Laertes left and spoke to Hamlet in the hallway, Polonius hid himself—with Mother's consent—so he could hear what was said.

She had consented to let this man spy on him. Their first private meeting since he came home, and she had asked Polonius to stay and spy. What did she think that Hamlet would do?

I killed a man. A good and decent man, who served his king and queen well.

No, *she* killed him. By ordering him to spy on her son, she killed him. By calling out for help that she didn't need, she killed him. Did she think he would *ever* raise his hand against her? Apparently she did. And now Polonius was dead because of it.

"Tell King Claudius," said Hamlet. "I will bear whatever penalty he sets for me. It was my hand killed him. A mistake—but the mistake was his, hiding behind a curtain in my mother's chamber. How could he imagine this would end?"

Hamlet turned to his mother, who still sat on the floor, her face stricken. "I know what you are; what you never understood was what *I* am."

"You know nothing," she said.

"If that's true," he said, "whose fault is that?"

He left the room, still holding his dagger. If he had passed King Claudius on the way, he would have put the blade in him on the spot. But Claudius was protected, for the moment, and Hamlet found his way out into the graveyard again, still holding the bloody dagger. Horatio was gone. He saw no one. He plunged the dagger into the grass and dirt of Yorick's grave, and washed it with the damp of the grass and wiped it on his own doublet.

He could hear the tumult in the castle. A woman screaming. Men shouting. But no soldiers came for him. Mother must be standing with the story of its being an accident. She was honest enough to know that the fault was hers, and would not accuse him of murder.

Too little honesty, too late. Poor Polonius. An old fool, dead for doing what kings and queens commanded.

And then a strange, exhilarating thought:

I've killed a man. It was easy. As natural as breathing. Now there's nothing stopping me from doing what must be done.

It was as if he heard his father's voice, that deep spectral sound that had shivered him to the soul that night on the battlements: Good, my son. Well done, my son. Hurry up and finish it, my son.

It came more quickly than he thought it would. By torchlight, in the great hall.

Hamlet was in the garden where his father had died. Horatio brought him his sword. "Laertes is looking for you," he said.

"I don't have time for Laertes. He must know I didn't mean to kill his father," said Hamlet.

"It's not his father," said Horatio. "It's his sister."

"Ophelia? I didn't touch her."

"She killed herself. Walked out into the sea, dressed in her heaviest gown. A funeral gown. Two soldiers went in after her, and a boat was launched, but when they brought her body back, she was dead."

"And for that he wants to kill me?"

"He blames you. Between killing her father and trifling with her affections—"

"I don't want to fight Laertes."

"Hamlet—he's been practicing for four years in order to fight you."

"What? We were friends! Until this afternoon I thought we still were!"

"It's not what you think. He meant to kill your father. But he believed that in order to kill him, he'd have to fight you first. He knew that nobody could beat you with a sword—but he was determined to try. Now your father is dead, but his rage isn't. If you leave, just stay away for a few days—take ship for the Orkneys, Hamlet, I beg you to do it. Laertes will be back in his right mind before you return."

"But I won't be," said Hamlet. "My father is unburied."

"He's also dead," said Horatio. "You aren't, and so far neither is Laertes."

"And neither is Claudius."

"Exactly. Leave bad enough alone, Hamlet."

But Hamlet had already strapped on his sword and was striding toward the castle.

"O God!" cried Horatio. "Stop him! Stop this all!"

The torches flickered and danced. Several courtiers were already there, as were the king and queen. Laertes was pacing up and down in front of them, shouting, demanding justice, vengeance, satisfaction. "My sister's dead body is still drenched in seawater and I'll have the heart's blood of the rogue who drowned her!"

"No one drowned her but herself," said King Claudius.

It galled Hamlet to hear his uncle plead for him. "Enough talk!" he cried from the far end of the chamber. "Do you want my heart, Laertes? You had it all our lives, it still belongs to you. Take it now, if you can!"

Their swords drawn, they fairly flew at each other across the room, blades flashing. Everyone moved out of the way, behind the arches, trusting in the stone pillars that held up the ceiling to keep them safe.

How many times had they fought, as boys? Laertes had learned much since then. There was no playfulness about it now. Laertes' every blow and thrust was intended to kill or maim; he moved in a fury, taking no pause for breath.

Yet Hamlet saw very quickly that Laertes could not win unless he let him. It was not a lack of skill—Laertes was as good a swordsman as Hamlet had ever seen. Nor was it Laertes' rage: He fought with control, with a furious calm that made no mistakes.

He simply wasn't quick enough. All his practice and study with the sword in France had made him an interesting opponent, but not one that could defeat Hamlet, even with his lack of practice. Laertes had new and clever moves that Hamlet

had not seen before; but he understood them at once and countered them and that was it.

"Laertes, stop this," Hamlet said. "You aren't good enough. You won't win."

"Then I'll die," said Laertes. "I have nothing left but this. You've taken it all from me."

"I've taken nothing from you. I grieve at your father's death. Your sister's suicide destroys me. I cared for her as much as I could for any woman, and I wished no harm on either of them. Nor do I wish to hurt you."

"Kill me or die," said Laertes.

"The only way I'll die is if you poisoned your blade and some of it spills on me," said Hamlet.

Laertes' answer was a furious onslaught. But he drew no blood. He didn't even nick the clothing Hamlet wore.

Hamlet maneuvered the fight so that his back was to his mother and King Claudius.

"I have only one enemy in this room," said Hamlet, "and it isn't you. It's the man who killed my father, married his widow, and stole the crown."

He could hear people gasping at his words. And Mother cried out, "He didn't! It's a lie! Who told you such a thing!"

Hamlet gave a twist and a spin and Laertes' sword flew up to the ceiling and then clattered back down a dozen yards away. With his opponent disarmed, Hamlet whirled on King Claudius.

"The ghost of my father told me!" cried Hamlet. "How you poured poison in his ear while he lay asleep in the garden! I swore an oath to avenge him, and this day I honor my father's command!"

Uncle Claudius was rising to his feet—to fight? to flee? it mattered not a whit. For Hamlet ran him through the heart and had the sword back out again in time to whirl and face

Laertes, who was running at him from behind, his sword again in hand.

There was not time for finesse. With Claudius's blood still hot on the blade, it went through Laertes' heart as well.

"No!" cried Hamlet.

"O God!" cried Horatio. "O God, how could you punish them all for my sin!"

"Your sin?" said Hamlet.

"I killed your father!"

Hamlet stared at him dumbfounded. Horatio, unarmed, tore open his shirt. "Here's my heart! Kill me! I'm the one you vowed to murder to avenge your father! I'm the one who killed him!"

Hamlet staggered back, turned a little, touched his uncle, who lay sprawled across the table while Mother wept over him.

"But Father said—"

"He lied! The old bastard lied!" cried Horatio. "Why didn't you tell me what he said? I would have told you. I thought you knew the truth—I offered to let you kill me right there in the garden! I thought you understood!"

"Offered? But I never—why would *you* kill him?"

"Because he was evil. Because of what he did to us. All of us. The Companions. All the boys but you!"

Behind him, Hamlet heard his mother wail.

"What did he do?" asked Hamlet.

"He had us," said Horatio. "All of us, one by one, over and over again. Told us how much we owed him. Our duty to the king. How to thank him."

"Thank him?"

"With our bodies! You've never heard of such a thing? You read the Greeks and Romans and you never heard of it?"

"But you never told me."

"He swore he'd kill us if we told."

"All of you?"

"It twisted us. I saw it in the others. Rosencrantz and Guildenstern, they could never look at women. Laertes—he told me, even before he left for France, that his stick was broken and would never grow again. And me—I thought I was all right. I thought…"

He broke down and wept.

Mother's voice came from behind him. "When I found what he was doing to the Companions, I almost killed him myself. I caught him fondling you when you were practically a baby, Hamlet. I held a knife at his throat and vowed that I'd have his blood if he ever touched you or was alone with you again. I'd tell the barons and they'd kill him themselves. He took a solemn oath never to touch you and he kept it. I didn't know what he did with the Companions until—until Laertes came to me and told. Then I made him dissolve the Companions and let them all go free. But it was too late."

"Too late," echoed Horatio. "A few months ago, a new page came to the castle. I taught him. He followed me everywhere like a dog. I delighted in his company. And then one day I found myself…I had him naked, I was telling him how a boy shows love to his friend and teacher…the words your father used, the very words. I was the worst of all of them! I was *like him*! I stopped myself. I told the boy to dress and never come near me again. That I was evil. A monster. And then I went out into the garden to kill your father. There he was, asleep. As if the devil had a right to rest in such a place! I took my dagger and poised it over him. Then with my other hand I clamped his mouth closed, holding his head in place, and then I pushed the dagger down into his ear and through his brain. He twitched, he pissed, he shat, he died. And that's where your mother and Claudius found me. I was working up the courage to put the knife into my own heart. They took it from me, and then your mother washed the blood as best she could and Claudius and I carried the body to the icehouse and wrapped it. Hamlet, it was me."

"He said it was poison in his ear."

"The blade must have felt cold at first, and then it burned going in," said Horatio. "He never turned his face. He never saw."

"But spirits...don't they *know*?"

"Maybe he did," said Horatio. "But he wanted Claudius dead because he was the *king* your father never knew how to become. He lied to you! He used you as surely as he used the rest of us!"

"What have I done," whispered Hamlet.

"Your father's ghost appeared to you?" said Mother.

"He said that Claudius..."

"I know the things he'd say," she said. "Oh, the liar. The monster. I should have killed him when I could. Better to have my hands stained with a husband's blood than all the evil that has come from letting him survive!" She fumbled for something in the waistband of her dress. "It was my fault, all of it!" she said. "I should have denounced him to the barons!"

She found what she was looking for—a small phial. Before Hamlet could reach to stop her, she had it open and drank it down.

"I love you, Hamlet," she said. "I tried to protect you. Horatio did only what I should have done. What the law of God demanded." Then the poison struck and she cried out in agony. She threw herself upon the body of King Claudius, cried out his name, and died.

Hamlet turned to face Horatio, who was still standing there, bare-chested, head bowed, waiting for the blade.

"Keep your oath," said Horatio. "Kill the killer of your father."

"If you had told me," said Hamlet. "If I'd known, do you think I'd have shed a drop of blood to avenge him?"

Hamlet knelt beside Laertes. "What my father meant to do to me, he did to you instead, my friend. All my friends. And now how many suffered, and how many died, to protect me from the monster whose blood half-fills my veins?"

Then he staggered to his feet and went to his mother's body, which lay half overspreading Claudius's. "Mother, you did for me what you could; you thought it was enough; and it was. He never touched me. And you, Uncle Claudius, what a good king you were. You should have been king all along. I would to God you had been my father."

Hamlet was still holding the sword, but when he turned again to Horatio, he let it fall. "I forbid you to die," he said to Horatio. "You are the one good man still living. You did justice on a devil. You served me well, and the king, and the kingdom. I command you to live. When Fortinbras comes, hail him king of Denmark. Let the kingdoms be united. Tell him that he has the vengeance he long wanted, and now I charge him to be a good king to Norse and Danes alike."

"Tell him yourself."

"My father deserved to die," said Hamlet. "There was no sin in what you did. But how will the deaths of my mother and my uncle and good Laertes and Polonius and Ophelia be avenged? If only I had let Laertes kill me. But I didn't, and now his blood joins the others."

"You're innocent of any wrong," said Horatio.

"God gave me only one gift—to know how to handle a blade. Too bad it took me this long to learn where the point of it most needed to be put."

Then Hamlet drew his dagger and pushed it, smoothly, unhesitatingly, into his own chest, between the ribs, just beside the breastbone. It found his heart—he felt it as a searing agony. He heard it as a song.

As he fell to his knees, he could hear Horatio weeping. "Live," Hamlet whispered one last time.

"I will," said Horatio. "Ah, Hamlet, I love you!"

Then Hamlet's body slumped onto the floor.

But his spirit did not go where his body went. His spirit arose and looked around the hall. To where Laertes' spirit held his father's and his sister's hands; then they arose into heaven. To where his mother and Claudius, bright spirits both, embraced each other, and also rose into the air, toward the bright light awaiting them.

And finally to the dark shadowy corner where his father's spirit stood, laughing, laughing, laughing. "Welcome to Hell, my beautiful son. At last we'll be together as I always longed for us to be."